READY, AIM, WOOF!

A TAMSIN KERNICK ENGLISH COZY MYSTERY

BOOK 2

LUCY EMBLEM

CHAPTER ONE

The song *Always look on the bright side of life!* burst into Tamsin's dreams. She stretched out an arm and flapped her hand about trying to locate her phone to switch off the alarm. Subsiding back onto her pillow with a sigh, eyes closed, she got her second, more violent, wake-up call.

Moonbeam had hopped onto the bed and was giving Tamsin's sleepy face a wash, her tail swishing fast in her delight at the new day.

"Ok, dogs, give me a minute," drawled Tamsin as she ruffled her dark hair and swept it off her face, turning her head away from the licking and reaching out to touch the heads of Quiz and Banjo who had also come to the side of the bed to greet her, Quiz's tail thumping the radiator with a whoosh-clang, whoosh-clang noise.

She could see through the crack between the curtains that it was a bright June day, but it wasn't going to be hot.

"You can come in the van today!" she said to her happy gang, who had no idea what she was talking about, but were glad to go along with it and waved their tails more vigorously.

A while later she was making coffee in the kitchen when the goddess-like Emerald, yawning loudly, came floating down the stairs - her white-blonde hair pouring down her back like a shimmering waterfall - along with the dot-dot-dot sound of her equally gorgeous white cat, Opal, padding softly ahead of her, hopping down each step.

"I don't need an alarm clock in this place," smiled Emerald as she came to inspect the coffee mugs and get some food out for Opal, who was already standing on the worktop next to her empty bowl, her bushy tail swishing impatiently.

"Are you suggesting I'm noisy?"

"Not you - the tails! The noise goes through all the pipework in the house."

"A secret message from Quiz!"

"Yes. And, deciphered, it reads 'Get up'." She just had time to withdraw the spoon from Opal's bowl as the cat settled down on her haunches, purring, to eat her breakfast.

"It's all part of the service," smiled Tamsin, handing her a mug of steaming coffee. "Doing much today?"

"Oh just the usual Tuesday, a couple of private yoga sessions and the Dynamic Flow class at the Cake Stop tonight. I thought I'd drop into the Buddhist temple at lunchtime for a meditation session."

"Malvern is just the strangest place! There really is something for everyone, but more if you are Hippie-inclined, I think."

"Good place, yes! What about you?" Emerald nibbled a strawberry.

"Got three home visits - two new puppies, and one dog growling over his food. No class today - had one at Nether Trotley last night."

"Oh yes, how did it go? It's amazing that those classes seem to have taken off!" Emerald's surprise was due to the inauspicious start to Tamsin's classes at that new venue, only a month or two ago.

"It went great! Eight students, all keen as mustard. I guess it brings out the ghoulish side of people's natures, their curiosity. I shan't complain - I'm fully booked right into August!"

"So it's an ill wind that blows nobody any good," smiled Emerald, looking up from her coffee.

They both paused for a moment as they thought of the unfortunate person for whom the wind had blown very ill indeed, and both sighed. Tamsin, reaching for her pot of prepared sausage and cheese treats from the fridge, said, "I'm off. It's cool enough, so I'll take the dogs. See you later ..."

Loading her training bag and the three dogs into her van, Tamsin smiled as she slid the door shut and found herself gazing at the words *Top Dogs* emblazoned on the side of the van. It had taken her a while to fulfil her dream of working with dogs all day, and she felt a warm glow as she hopped into the van and left Pippin Lane behind. Tamsin drove along the back roads towards Hereford, looking out for the turn-off for Bishop's Green, and as always, noting the location of the brown public footpath signs that formed part of her ever-expanding mental map of dog walks. Though sunny, the day was cool, as a light breeze waved the smaller tree branches and the cow parsley in the hedgerow. The dog roses and the bramble flowers peeped out from the hawthorn hedges, jostling for sunny positions.

"*There's* a good place for us for later, guys," she called into the back of the van as she passed a signpost next to the little bridge they had just driven over. "Looks like the path follows the river - you'll like that!"

And after going twice round Bishop's Green she at last found The White House ("You can't miss it," Verena had said on the phone. "It's just after the red brick wall," her husband Mike had chipped in, though he'd clearly forgotten that the wall had been painted yellow since they first moved in). The house overlooked the large Green itself, big enough for a cricket match with its small wooden Victorian pavilion at one end, and accommodating a pond at the other. Tamsin wondered how many cricket balls had been lost in that pond (and whether it counted as a four or a six ...) as she found a large shady chestnut tree - its tiny conkers still in their green spiky jackets - to park the van under and set off on her first assign-ment of the day. She saw there was a notice on the tree, but hoping it didn't say "No parking", she didn't stop to read it.

Tamsin loved her sessions with brand new puppies! They were such fun that she sometimes felt *she* should be paying the owners rather than the other way round. Showing them how to get great results with their little pup without ever having to say "No" was a joy. And this visit was no different.

It wasn't long before this little Jack Russell puppy - who was only nine weeks old - had completely run out of steam and fallen fast asleep to process all his new learning. So the remainder of the lesson was conducted over a coffee at the kitchen table.

Verena bustled about making the coffee, her flowered skirt swishing about her ample hips, as Mike, tall and quiet, sat at the table with Tamsin, going over their homework sheets and asking advice on the best place to site Bingo's crate - now occupied by the comatose puppy. Verena brought their drinks over to the old-fashioned scrubbed deal table and they fell to chatting.

"You should get plenty of business round here," volunteered Verena. "Everyone has a dog."

"Or dogs," added Mike.

"And some of them do need a bit of bringing to heel."

Tamsin winced at the old-fashioned expression - it was the antithesis of the way she worked. Nevertheless she smiled at Verena. "They have to want to make a change - like you did."

"I'll tell them! I'll tell everybody how wonderful you are. I can't believe how you stopped Bingo jumping all over you without appearing to do *anything*."

"And his tail never stopped wagging!" Mike smiled broadly.

"Thank you! I'd love to work with some of your neighbours."

"If Verena says she'll tell them - they'll be told! We're a very close-knit community here. Most have lived here for .. generations. We're the blow-ins, only been here fourteen years," Mike threw his head back and laughed.

"And they've always welcomed us, right from the start. Lovely folk."

"But there is a bit of a brouhaha at the moment," Mike offered.

"Development," Verena added.

Tamsin waited expectantly to see who was going to tell the story. It was Mike.

"Did you notice the row of slightly ramshackle cottages on the right as you came into the Green?"

Tamsin nodded slowly, trying to locate them in her memory from her trip twice round the village.

"Well, there's five of them in a row, and they have those long gardens at the back - each one has an acre. The old landlord died and his family who live the other end of the country wanted shot of them. They're planning to sell them to a developer who's looking for permission to demolish the lot and build a group of high-end homes on the land."

"He'll make a killing!" said Verena.

"And this is unpopular?"

Bingo yawned loudly, stretched, and rolled onto his back, four feet in the air, to continue his snooze, causing them all to look over and smile fondly at the puppy.

"I'll say," they both nodded vigorously as Verena went on, "there's a section of the Parish Council who are violently opposed. That sort of 'cottage on an acre' is the backbone of villages like this. 'Affordable housing' they'd call it these days, where people can be relatively self-sufficient. Low-cost living. Half the village is up in arms."

"Not to mention the five residents and their families who'll be evicted. Some of them have lived in those cottages for generations!"

"The proposed housing would attract well-off people who would work in Hereford or Worcester. They wouldn't be part of the fabric. We have a mid-sized house here, but we do both work from home much of the time, and we have chickens on our patch. We're on the committee of the local horticultural society - always been involved, you know? There's a lot of campaigning going on - did you see the posters?"

"Ah yes," the penny dropped about the notice where she'd parked, "I did."

"There's going to be a public meeting at the Village Hall next week. And the protestors here are getting rent-a-crowd in .."

"She means the people who had a similar plan rejected - in a little village over Trumpet way. They want to learn what they did, so they can get a better chance of overturning this application."

"Could get noisy!" said Verena, grinning with obvious relish.

At that moment the back door burst open, banging loudly against the dresser, and a man appeared in the doorway. They all turned to look at the uninvited visitor, Mike pushing back his chair and jumping to his feet, a thunderous expression clouding his face.

The man - about thirty and wearing a suit - stood white-faced and flustered. "I .. I .." he began, wringing his hands. Then, as quickly as he'd arrived, he turned on his heel and fled.

Mike ran to the door and watched the figure disappearing out to the road, before shutting it and flipping the Yale lock closed.

"What on earth ..?" said Verena, shocked.

"Do you know him?" asked Tamsin.

"No!" she said,

"Never seen him before," added Mike, returning slowly to his seat.

"Do you think he thought he was somewhere else, then when he looked inside he got disoriented?" Verena's brow furrowed with anxiety. "Should we go after him and see if he's alright?"

"He'd already disappeared. Presumably driven off by now ..."

"He looked terrified!" said Tamsin. "I wonder what could have happened."

"He did - that's one reason I watched him leave. There's nobody out there - that I could see."

"Why didn't Bingo bark?" asked Verena. "Is he going to be a useless watchdog?"

"He's just a baby. Don't worry - his guarding instincts will kick in when he's grown a bit, then you'll be pleading with me to stop him barking!"

Verena laughed, then her face clouded again. "That was very strange."

"Weird ... and look at the time! I must be off," Tamsin collected her things together. "Remember to follow the Housetraining Guide exactly! I'll see you again on Thursday."

"Look forward to it," smiled Verena as she clasped Tamsin's hand warmly.

"Is it ok if I leave the van where it is while I take my dogs along that footpath by the bridge?"

"Of course! That's a lovely walk. We're looking forward to walking there with Bingo in a few weeks." Verena looked fondly at the puppy, still stretched out on his back, dead to the world.

And off Tamsin went, looking carefully about her for strange men, as she gathered up her three dogs and set off to enjoy the delightful riverside walk.

CHAPTER TWO

"It was absolutely lovely! There was a huge area of Yellow Flags flowering - and the pretty Ladysmock just finishing." Tamsin licked the last crumbs off her fork and set it back on the plate. "Charity, you'd love it - and so would Muffin."

Sitting opposite her in The Cake Stop, Charity - her little tan fluffy dog Muffin on her lap as usual - nodded happily as a burst of laughter from a nearby table filled the busy cafe, its rich coffee aroma permeating the atmosphere. Though a considerably older woman - an old woman, in fact, with her neat grey bob and sensible clothes - Charity was spry and busy and had become a firm fan of Tamsin's work at her dog school. In fact, she'd been instrumental in solving the Nether Trotley mystery.

"It's like a picture postcard - the little bridge, the river, weeping willows, rushes, I even saw a kingfisher!"

"It sounds wonderful! I'm surprised I haven't come across it before - but it *is* the Hereford side of Malvern, while I'm the Gloucester side."

"Tell you what, Charity, I'm back there on Thursday morning - fancy joining me for a walk? You can pull in on the lay-by just past the bridge. It's a turn-off from the Trumpet road."

They were just arranging the time and place as Jean-Philippe strolled over to greet them both, his tea-towel thrown over his shoulder as always.

"*Mesdames! Bonjour!*" he bowed with a flourish. "And how are you both today? Hatching more plans?"

"Yes, we're going on a dog walk together."

Jean-Philippe leant to scratch Muffin's ear, then bent further to offer his hand to Banjo, beside Tamsin. Shy Banjo recognised the hand's owner and thumped his tail softly once before turning away again. "You ladies live dangerously," he smiled and started to collect their empty crockery.

"No Kylie today?" asked Tamsin, peering past the displays to the empty serving area.

"Dentist. She'll be in shortly. I hope before the lunchtime rush. The Furies are dropping in later - at least it's usually just Damaris who does the delivering - cos we're very low on cakes. And their latest Passionfruit Meringue Extravaganza is right out."

Tamsin smiled with pleasure as she thought of the three indomitable Dodds sisters, known fondly as the Three Furies to friends and customers alike. Penelope, Electra, and Damaris were three remarkably contrasting characters from another age, looking like something out of *Gormenghast*, yet running a highly successful commercial catering business from their Victorian villa on the side of the Malvern Hills.

"Are you planning any more of your big dog walks?" asked Jean-Philippe. The last one was .. pretty eventful, *n'est-ce pas?*"

"Don't remind me!" Tamsin cast her eyes heavenwards, remembering how worried she'd been about the future of her business, as the Nether Trotley Mystery plot had thickened. "But I will, yes. It was great fun - well, until ... you know - and it did lead to a surge in sign-ups for me. I thought we may venture onto the Hills for the next one."

"Sounds lovely, dear!" said Charity. "May I help on the day?"

"You most certainly may, you're so good at dealing with problems, or .. happenings."

"There won't be any 'happenings' this time. It'll just be fun, you mark my words."

Jean-Philippe gave the table a last wipe with his cloth before attempting to flip it back over his shoulder. But it fell to the floor and was instantly scooped up by Muffin, who'd hopped off Charity's lap and sat proudly holding it for him.

"Why, *merci ma petite!*" he said, accepting the tea-towel. "That's a useful trick," he said to Charity.

"Ooh yes, Tamsin's got us learning lots of tricks!" she enthused. "I started by getting her to pick up a cloth - I'm always dropping them - and holding it nicely. I drop them on purpose now, just so she can do her trick!"

"You know what you'd enjoy teaching her?" Tamsin leaned forward in her chair, "Get her to hold your cuff, so she can pull your coat off for you."

"Oh, we'd love that, wouldn't we Muffmuff? We'll start as soon as I'm home. I'll use my old gardening coat, it's quite baggy. What a good idea! Useful too, now I'm getting older and stiffer."

"Just teach one step at a time - like you have with the cloth."

"So I start by offering her the cuff?"

"Yes, don't be wearing the coat yet - just hold the sleeve out."

"And when she's doing that I start putting it on?"

"Ye-e-e-s, but get the first bit going and then we can look at the next step. Perhaps next Monday in class."

Jean-Philippe draped the towel - successfully this time - over his shoulder and said, "Emerald was in a bit earlier - you just missed her."

"Was she sorting the upper room for her class tonight?"

"*Mais non,* she was just here to eat *gateau.*"

"The beast!" exclaimed Tamsin. "I tell you, this cake I've just had will be on my hips by tomorrow morning. I'll be struggling to fasten my trousers. And Emerald just looks like a wraith, whatever she eats."

"We are all different," said Charity sagely.

"And we must all allow ourselves to enjoy the good things in life!" added Jean-Philippe with a grin as he turned back to the counter with the tray.

"Well, I will certainly enjoy the riverside walk on Thursday, Charity - especially as I'll be walking off a few more mouthfuls!"

"You're perfect as you are, dear, and you are so active. 'Comparison is the thief of joy,' don't they say?"

"They do."

"Enjoy your life as well as your cake!"

"I'll do that! Right, well I'm off now, got another couple of home visits to do today, then reports to write up ..." Tamsin rose, gathering up Banjo's lead and putting his mat back in her bag. "See you tomorrow!"

And as she went through the heavy glass door of the cafe, with "The Cake Stop" etched on the glass in Art Nouveau-style lettering, she looked back fondly at the familiar scene, Jean-Philippe waving cheerily to her, as Charity was already chatting to a couple at another table.

"Really, is there anyone Charity doesn't know?" she wondered, and set off for her van.

CHAPTER THREE

Bingo was excited to see his new friend when Tamsin arrived once more at The White House the next day. Verena had been doing her homework with him and he was responding well to the games. "And thanks to your Housetraining Guide he's already lasting the night now, so we're all sleeping like babies!"

"For that we are forever in your debt," smiled Mike. "I've been tied up at work a lot," he was at pains to point out, "so that's why I haven't done anything much with Bingo. I do play with him though!"

Nothing new there, thought Tamsin. The women tend to be the nurturers while the men go out in their bearskins and fight dinosaurs, real or imagined. But then she thought about Maggie and Don - other clients of hers, both doctors, who actually lived only a few miles from Verena and Mike, and how it was Don who did most of the work with Jez. The exception that proves the rule.

"Play is what it's all about!" she encouraged Mike. "As long as the play has rules."

"To stop him getting too rough and bitey?"

"Just to lay down guidelines. Like *we* do with our games. Imagine a tennis game. Wouldn't work if one person insisted on hitting all the balls out over the fence! Here, let me show you ..." and she started the lesson, teaching Bingo how to play excitedly with the tug and instantly let go again when asked. Mike watched fascinated and was eager to take his turn.

Bingo lasted a bit longer this time, as they'd taken care to have him rested before the session, and he learnt lots of new things. "He's a bright little thing," Tamsin told the smiling owners, as he sat before her, ears pricked, eyes shining. But once he started to fade they practised his bedtime routine, and there was still time to sit round the table at the end with coffee - proper coffee, with cream: irresistible!

"I've got two numbers for you to ring." Verena said proudly as she handed Tamsin her mug. "There's Lionel with his young Labrador. He's a big softy but has a tendency to wander. They're up at the Manor." She offered biscuits, but Tamsin steeled herself and declined. "Then there's Julia. She's got a dog that drags her round the village. She daren't let him off the lead because he barks at everything he sees and she's afraid he'll bite someone."

"Right up my alley!" said Tamsin with a broad smile. "Thank you - I'll give them a ring when I get back." She stowed the scrap of paper carefully in her training bag. "Any more from your mystery visitor?"

"No, nothing," said both of them, still looking as baffled the day it had happened..

Verena went on, "I asked around and no-one else had seen him. I wonder if he was something to do with the development. He was wearing a suit, not country gear."

"A surveyor, perhaps? Aren't they the first on the scene usually?" asked Tamsin.

"Doesn't account for his dashed odd behaviour," grunted Mike.

"If he *is* to do with the development project, then presumably he'll be back."

"Hopefully not here!" said Verena with feeling.

"Well, we'll doubtless find out next week," said Mike.

"Of course, the meeting! Yes darling, I suppose he'll be there if he's involved."

"How is the level of village ferment?" Tamsin asked with a grin.

"Oh, brewing nicely," smiled Verena, who clearly had a naughty streak. "I'm not involved directly. Like to keep my head down. But if there's a vote I'll definitely be voting against."

"The cottages *are* old and tatty." Mike conceded. "But it's important that this kind of property should be available. We've already lost our school. Getting rid of the ordinary folk can kill a village. It could just become a dormitory for the nearest towns."

"So you don't mind those cottages going, as long as they're replaced with something similar?" asked Tamsin tentatively.

"But then people have developed their gardens," protested Verena before Mike could speak. "They've planted trees, tilled the land. Old Pru Cunningham made a big pond. It's quite a draw for herons and apparently there's lots of wildlife that needs a pond."

"And watery plants too, I imagine," said Tamsin.

"I think the residents are quite happy with their tumbledown properties. They're the sort of people who took on those places because of the land attached. They *use* the land. They don't just put ornaments in it and boring shrubs to fill the space."

"If you don't count Major Cooper-Johnson's 'ornaments'!" laughed Mike. Seeing Tamsin's perplexed expression he said, "You'll see when you visit Julia. He lives next door to her."

Tamsin, wondering what kind of collection of garden gnomes Major Cooper-Johnson must have, made her goodbyes and left, fixing the next date for Bingo's learning program.

She hurried to the van, realising she was running late. "Come on dogs, we'll drive," she said as she jumped in, the walls of the van clanging with the tails thudding against them. "Oh Lord, Charity's always early - I hope she's not wandering around looking for us."

But as Tamsin drew up behind Charity's little blue car in the lay-by, she saw the road was almost blocked with police cars, lights flashing. Charity was not to be seen.

"Oh no! What's happened? Here, you stay here a moment," she said to her dogs, who were impatiently waiting for their walk to begin.

She ran across the road, past the first police car and was smartly intercepted by a uniformed policeman.

"Sorry miss, you can't come this way."

"But my friend ... Is she alright? What's happened?"

"Can you describe your friend, Miss?"

"Er, she's about seventy, small, got a little brown dog .."

"Female?" queried the constable.

"Very definitely. So is her owner." Tamsin glared at him as he raised an eyebrow. "Is she alright? I must go to her ..."

"Yes, she's alright, but she's helping us with our enquiries." He trotted out the familiar phrase.

"Enquiries into what?"

"There's been an incident .."

At that moment Tamsin could see over his shoulder a tearful Charity clinging to Muffin's lead, being led along the path towards the cars. Tamsin thought fast and let out a loud shout of *"Woof!"* Her van burst into a frenzy of barking. She pushed past the distracted policeman and ran towards her friend, followed by shouts of "Oi! Miss! You can't ..."

"Charity! What's happened?" Tamsin wrapped an arm round Charity's thin, shaking, shoulders.

"There's a man," wailed Charity, with a hand pressed to her face.

"Excuse me Miss," said the policeman accompanying Charity. "Who are you, and why are you here?"

"I'm Tamsin Kernick and I was meeting Miss Cleveland here for a walk."

"I'll have to ask you to leave."

"But she needs me! Can't you see she's in shock?" Tamsin tightened her hold round Charity's shoulders. "What man?" she asked her.

"He's ... dead!" gasped the appalled Charity.

"Dead?"

"Dead," said the policeman. "And this lady is coming back with us to the station to help with our enquiries."

"That's ridiculous! Can't you just get her story here?"

"Sorry Miss. We have our protocols to adhere to."

"The first thing you should do is get the station doctor to see her. She's shocked! At the very least she needs a strong cup of tea. I'll come with you," she said to Charity.

"No you won't. She can ask for a solicitor if she wishes ..."

"You're arresting her?!" squawked Tamsin.

"Not yet. But she does have some questions to answer."

"Who's the man, Charity?"

"I've no idea, Tamsin dear - I just found him. Over there in the reeds," she pointed. "Well, Muffin did actually. I thought he'd just fallen. But then ... the arrows .." she started to sob.

"*Arrows?*" said Tamsin incredulously.

"One in his back, and some on the ground. I saw them as I walked down the path. The first one was sticking into the ground. Then there were two more lying flat. I thought they would be dangerous if children found them, so I picked them up as I walked."

"She was holding the weapons when we arrived."

Tamsin rolled her eyes heavenwards, "So who alerted the police?"

"Anonymous call. We arrived on the scene and found this lady holding a murder weapon."

"A murder weapon that needs a bow to fire it! Does this lady have a bow?" demanded Tamsin.

"We're searching the path and the bank now, Madam."

"I never heard anything so ridiculous. Can you get her to the doctor?" demanded Tamsin of the policeman in such a stern voice that he nodded agreement. And seeing the limp state of their suspect, he realised he'd better do just that.

"Here, Charity, I'll take Muffin. Let me know the moment they finish with you. Your car is fine here for a while. You'll be in no fit state to drive. The police will have to drive you home," she glowered imperiously at the policeman, now looking cowed in the face of this woman who was becoming more and more challenging.

And as they headed towards the road, Tamsin peeled off silently and crept back towards where a man was bending over a body. It was Don! He must be the nearest doctor and had been called out.

"Don!" she called quietly, as she approached him. One of the men combing the bank with a stick started towards her.

"It's alright Constable, she's with me," said Don, rising and intercepting her. "You'll need to scram, I'm afraid," he said quietly to her.

"I was curious. They've taken poor Charity. It's absurd ..."

"It is. Delightful old lady. I remember meeting her at your dog walk. But I'll be round to the station in a moment to attend to her officially. I already gave her a quick check over and she's ok."

"Who is this guy?" started Tamsin, then interrupted herself as she moved and caught a view of the dead man's face through the rushes. "I know him!" she whispered.

"You do?"

"No. I don't mean that. I don't *know* him. I mean I *saw* him the other day. A strange man ..."

"Then you need to tell the police."

"Not sure that's such a good idea ..."

"I think you should head home with your extra dog, and await a visit from them. They're just following procedure. They'll have to fingerprint your friend since she handled some of the arrows. I'll have them drive her home once I've seen her again."

"There's id on him?"

The doctor pointed to his case which had the corners of evidence bags peeping out. "We have his wallet. But everything will have to be checked."

The policeman who had been prodding the rushes with his stick came and stood close by, unsure which would be worse - incurring the wrath of the Doctor or the wrath of his Sergeant.

"I'll talk to you later, Don." Tamsin took the hint and went back to the van. She drove the dogs to another less exciting footpath on her mental map for a walk while she watched her phone for news from Charity and thought about what had happened.

And the first thing she thought was, "How come I've tripped over another body?" Though at least she didn't seem to be under suspicion herself this time! Verena and Mike would be able to give her an alibi -

assuming the attack only happened recently. She hadn't asked Don that - but maybe he couldn't have told her anyway. Oh no! Supposing it happened just before she arrived at the Green? Her mind raced - but for now poor Charity was definitely in the police sights.

"I must help her," she assured her dogs and the slightly anxious Muffin, and Banjo came and pressed his muzzle into her hand. "You have no idea what I'm talking about, Banjo, but you sure know when I need comfort!" She smiled to them all as they walked. And while the dogs sniffed every blade of grass and every leaf on their walk, Tamsin was so pre-occupied that she saw little.

CHAPTER FOUR

Tamsin had completed two more home visits - to a Great Dane who was joyfully ruling the house and pulling his tiny old lady owner flat on her face (why did people choose such unsuitable dogs? she thought to herself, then remembered that these poor choices were her bread and butter!) and another new puppy, a poor mite clearly many weeks older than the owners had been told - most probably from a puppy farm - who was afraid of his own shadow. So she was pleased to get home and check her messages and find one from Charity whom the police had indeed taken home.

"I'll be round with Muffin straight away," she assured her friend as she called her back. "Yes, she's fine. No, really, Charity, Muffin's had a great day with my lot. It's you I'm worried about ..."

But just as she was leaving with Muffin the phone rang. Concerned it may be Charity again, she turned back from the door and answered it.

"My dear!" gasped Verena in excitement, "*Have you heard* what's happened? Were you there? Did you see all the police cars? It was just after you left .. "

"I saw them," Tamsin found a gap to put in her answer, which was swiftly followed by a flood more questions from Verena.

"Have you ever heard of such a thing? It seems a man was killed by a madman with a bow and arrow! And do you know who it was? You won't believe this ... it was the mystery man, the one who burst into our home!"

Tamsin thought she'd keep quiet about having actually been on the scene, and said what was expected of her, "No! Really?"

"Yes! Really!" Verena was beside herself with excitement, and Tamsin remembered how keenly she'd been anticipating the local meeting in the hope of some aggro. "And do you know who he *actually* is?"

"No! Who?" Tamsin marvelled at the speed at which police classified information was getting round Bishop's Green.

"They *say* he's the chief surveyor - I mean he *was* the chief surveyor - of the company who'll be developing the cottages. It *seems*," she rushed on, "that there may have been some reason they wouldn't be able to build there. Something to do with watercourses, I don't know."

"So someone didn't want him to find that out? That's weird. Surely any surveyor would? They'd just send another."

"Or maybe someone was trying to warn off surveyors in general. Someone from the cottages, perhaps?" she added with a hint of mystery.

"What an awful thought! But that should be easy to find out, shouldn't it, someone who can find their way round a bow and arrow? There can't be many!"

"Ah, but that's where it's such a clever choice of weapon!" Verena said triumphantly. "Bishop's Green is the epicentre of archery in Herefordshire! It's where they hold the annual Field Archery Championship, on Lionel's land. Everyone here knows their way round a bow and arrow! They're *born* with a bow in their hand. Even I've had a go!"

Tamsin winced at that thought, then shuddered. Being involved in one murder mystery had been, she had hoped, the last time she'd have to deal with this. But it seems malevolence was following her about.

She promised to catch up with Verena on her next visit to Bingo in a couple of days.

"The village is in a ferment," added Verena with undisguised enthusiasm. "That meeting is going to be something else," she giggled, as she hung up.

Really, thought Tamsin, a man has been horribly killed, and she thinks it's all been laid on for her entertainment. She sighed, called Muffin again, and this time she really did leave.

Settling down with the cup of tea which Charity had ready for her when she arrived in Nether Trotley, Tamsin watched Muffin curl up happily in her usual lap with a sigh, and herself accepted the attentions of Sapphire, one of Charity's purring cats. "So. Tell all!"

"I have an inkling of how you felt over ... over that other business," she began. "You were under suspicion there because of being the first on the scene. And it seems there's some police manual that says whoever is first there - however unlikely - must be guilty. I should be glad they didn't arrest Muffin!"

Tamsin gazed at the biscuit she was being offered, which - after a quick debate with herself about the relative importance of friendship versus waistlines - she accepted.

"It wasn't true last time and it isn't true this time either," she took a chomp of the delicious crumbly, chocolatey, home-baked morsel. "Mmm, Charity, this is delicious!"

"Of course it's not true. And after being so stern and terrifying at the riverbank, they actually became quite pleasant once we got back onto their home ground. It was quite entertaining, in a way. I expected to have my fingers squashed into an ink pad like they used to show in films way back when, but I just had to touch a screen. It seems that Malvern has the very latest gadgets. And the results - that I was not on the Wanted list, no Interpol tag on my name - came back in seconds! Quite extraordinary."

"The wonders of modern technology!" laughed Tamsin, glad to be able to laugh at something.

"So what else did they do? Did you get to see Chief Inspector Hawkins?"

"No. Seems he was at the golf course. I overheard the desk sergeant saying that's where he's always to be found as he coasts towards retirement. I had a very stern-looking career policewoman and her sidekick.

They sat me down with a cup of lukewarm tea and asked lots of questions. Two of them, quick fire, jumping from one subject to another. Trying to catch me out I suppose. I may look dotty and old, but they soon found that I'm not!"

Tamsin grinned, "You're sure not!"

"I just kept saying the same thing - that I was waiting for you and spotted the arrows and picked them up. They're wood, but they've got a metal point on them. Dangerous! They shouldn't be left lying around for children to play with - could take an eye out! That's what I told them."

"So you collected them?"

"I did. I picked them up, then Muffin started barking, staring into the reeds, and I saw another arrow sticking up in the air, and ..."

"Got it. Don't see it again in your mind, Charity, it's ok. I wonder why there were all those arrows left there? And why so many missed the man, and then one hit him? Do you think there was a ghastly chase? Or ..." She stroked Sapphire pensively.

Charity spoke into the silence. "What is it, dear? What are you thinking?"

"Well, it seems that archery is The Thing in Bishop's Green. Everyone does it, and they hold big competitions there. So .. either someone who was no good at it was firing and missing, or .."

".. someone was missing on purpose to cover up the fact that they are an expert bowman!"

"Ye-e-es. It would have to narrow the field if someone was able to fell this guy with their first arrow. And maybe they were widening the field a little this way."

"What a devious thing you are, Tamsin! No wonder you cracked the Trotley case so fast!"

"In that case it was a question of finding out who wanted rid of someone. But here, it seems to be different - do you know who the victim is?"

"No? They didn't say."

"Well the bush telegraph has been singing, and it seems he was a surveyor, some say the Chief Surveyor for the company that wants to demolish a row of ancient cottages and put high-priced housing in their place. The plans have divided the village." And Tamsin explained the story to Charity, including what she knew and what Verena surmised.

"But they'll just send another surveyor, won't they?"

"Exactly what I thought. So either it was personal, or they were just warning off developers in general. It does seem extreme ... But .." she interrupted herself, "I haven't told you!"

Charity leant forward attentively, her hand on Muffin so she shouldn't slide off her lap.

"That man burst into the house I was teaching in a couple of days before, looking as if he had the hounds of hell on his tail. Maybe they were after him then too?"

"Poor man! Did he have a family?"

"No idea, I'm afraid. I hope not. He seemed rather pathetic."

"So we have people who are under threat of eviction from their homes," Charity mused. "We have villagers who don't want incomers who won't be part of the village."

"We have people who stand to make a lot of money out of the development ..." added Tamsin, "and a place swarming with archery experts!"

"Sounds like a case for Tamsin Kernick!" chortled Charity, patting Muffin.

"I didn't do it alone, you know," smiled Tamsin. "I had plenty of other people to bounce ideas off."

"We were all involved already. Then there was that nice young man Feargal, your journalist friend .."

"That's a point! I wonder how he's doing ... Listen, Charity - they're having a public meeting next week. We could go along - all of us - I'm sure Emerald would love to come, *and* Feargal - I'll put money on him already being on the trail!"

Charity clapped her hands with glee. "I'd love to! Nothing better than a rumpus in a village hall!"

"Fixed then. I'll get the details to you. And you need to collect your car too. Why don't we drive over there tomorrow and we can take a look at these famous cottages? There's someone I may have to call on there anyway. I have to ring her this evening."

"Wild horses!" beamed Charity, "wild horses wouldn't keep me away."

"So how long did you have to stay with the police after all?" Tamsin lowered the large, fluffy, and slightly indignant cat to the floor, and helped herself to another biscuit, while another cat hopped onto her lap to take Sapphire's place. She sighed, and continued her job of cat-stroking.

"When they saw I wasn't going to change my story, however many different questions they asked, that nice Doctor I met on your big dog walk checked me over again and told them to take me home. The constable who drove me back was quite apologetic. I think that a murder is a bit of an excitement for them in a calm and sedate place like Malvern, and they were anxious not to mess it up by missing some vital step. They must have been following the *Murder Manual for the Police Force*."

Tamsin smiled, then leant forward and peered at her friend. "You know what, Charity, you look quite done in. I think you should have an early night and get over the shock. Will you be alright here on your own?"

"I'm hardly on my own," Charity smiled back, indicating Muffin and her three cats. "I'll be fine. I'm not afraid here. But you're right - it's been an exhausting day, so I will turn in early."

"I'll be finding out more about the cottages and their denizens today and I'll ring you tomorrow with a time to pick you up to collect your car." And as she left, Tamsin felt a surge of rage within her for her old friend. "I don't care what the police say, I want your name absolutely cleared!" she called as she went down the path, picking her way through the riot of bright orange nasturtiums cascading over it.

Tamsin was on the case again!

CHAPTER FIVE

Once back home, Tamsin called the numbers Verena had given her, and fixed up to visit Lionel and his errant Labrador the next week. Julia, who lived in the famous cottages, was very anxious for her to visit as soon as possible. In fact she seemed altogether an anxious type, which doubtless contributed to her dog's anxiety, evidenced by the continual barking as they tried to speak.

"Perfect!" shouted Tamsin, "I'll see you and Romeo tomorrow at 10 o'clock! ... Yes, I'll look forward to meeting you too, and don't worry - Romeo will love it!"

"Is that one of these cottagers from Bishop's Green?" asked Emerald when the call was over.

"It is. And I'm dying to find out more! I'd hate it if someone tried to throw me out of my home. It was bad enough when Sebastian left and I thought I'd have to sell this place."

"Just as well your fairy godmother turned up at the right moment," beamed Emerald, who had come to share the house and its expenses shortly after Tamsin's break-up with her boyfriend.

"Very true. Verena said that Julia lives next to a mad Major who has lots of ornaments in his garden."

"Garden gnomes with fishing rods? Or statues of greek goddesses?"

"The mind boggles! I'll find out tomorrow. Hope this Julia is talkative - she seemed to be on the call just now. I'd love to learn more about all this."

"Nosy? Curious?"

"Yes. Both of those I have to admit. But there's also Charity to think of. She will feel a shadow over her till the real killer is caught."

"No-one in their right mind could imagine Charity mowing people down with arrows!" said Emerald with feeling.

"Of course not, but the shadow remains. Remember the awful things people were saying about me? No smoke without fire, kind of thing?"

"I do remember, yes. And it certainly put petrol on your flames of justice!"

"It did! I had to prove my innocence or it would all hang over me for ever. And the easiest way was to find out who really did it. Well, I feel the same now. For Charity."

"And it's fun."

"I have to confess ... it *is* exhilarating!" she giggled.

"Have you spoken to Feargal yet?" Emerald folded her long legs under her as she nursed a coffee mug with one hand, and her cat Opal on her knee with the other.

"Mind-reader! He's next on my list. Had to ring those possible new clients first."

"He'll love all this. Why don't you have him round for supper and fill him in on everything you know so far. His journalist brain will have plenty of stuff to go digging into."

And so Tamsin's day was firmly mapped out for Friday. First she was off to Bishop's Green to take Charity to collect her car, and to visit Julia and her barking Romeo, then back to Malvern for her Friday afternoon puppy class - always one of Tamsin's favourite hours of the week - and back for supper with Emerald and Feargal.

"There are so many villages and hamlets that I haven't yet discovered," said Charity as they travelled the back roads to Bishop's Green, the luscious scent of the cow parsley covering the verges and hedgerows flooding in the open windows of Tamsin's van.

"And this is one of them?"

"Now I think of it, I had heard mention of the Field Archery Championship. I just never connected it. Funny, the things that grow up in certain places - an enthusiast must have started it, and it just caught on."

"Pretty harmless pursuit I would guess. But don't they use those red, white and blue targets? I mean, they don't actually kill real animals, do they?"

"I don't know. Surely not? Wouldn't have thought so ... Perhaps you'll find out today?"

"I'm hoping to find out *lots* today!" smiled Tamsin as she pulled up in the lay-by behind Charity's little blue car. "Here you are. I'll wait to check it starts up ok, then I'll leave you to it."

"Thank you my dear." Charity glanced across to the footpath sign by the bridge, still sporting police tape strung across to the hedge, guarding the entrance to the path. "Maybe one day we'll feel brave enough for that walk. Such a pretty place."

"And maybe ... not. There are plenty of other walks. I'll find one without any bodies or bad memories for us to enjoy," laughed Tamsin as Charity shut the van door and set off for her car.

A couple of moments later, as they exchanged cheery toots, Charity made a turn and pulled away from the lay-by and Tamsin set off again to drive on to the cottages, eager to meet Julia and her noisy Romeo.

She parked outside No.1 and looked back along the row of old cottages. There were five of them, spaced out with about forty yards of frontage each, and past the tangled and colourful cottage garden in front of Julia's house a drive led down the side to the land at the back. She could see all the way down the grassy field to the row of small trees at the bottom - Alders and Willows, by the looks of them - giving away the secret of the stream at their feet.

The houses were all very similar - five small cottages crouched beneath their tiled rooves, with their brown rubble walls of characteristic higgledy-piggledy Malvern Stone, each with a front gate and drive. Some of the front doors were painted a faded dark green, though Julia had brightened hers with a coat of pale blue paint.

The front gardens were each very different! While Julia had a riot of traditional cottage garden flowers and vegetables mixed together, Tamsin could see that no.5, down at the far end, boasted an orderly and well-kept front garden of vegetable rows and runner bean cane wigwams.

No.3 was nondescript, while no.4 was looking sadly neglected, the grass too long, the gravel with weeds growing in it.

No.2 was the one she was keen to see though, from what had been hinted at by Verena and Mike - and it left her aghast!

Lurking amongst the shrubs and small trees were lifesize model animals - a badger, a turkey, three pigeons on a branch. As she looked more carefully she could see a gazelle, what may have been a red deer, and a huge bear waving its paws near the glossy royal blue-painted front door. It was while she was gazing at these that she heard the door of no.1 open and a small mousy-haired woman emerged looking flustered, a loudly-yapping dog beside her.

"Romeo, quiet!" she said crossly, and shouted, "Oh sorry - Tamsin, is it?" She bent over the barking dog, "Shhh!"

"Yes, I'm Tamsin - glad to meet you Julia! What a lovely garden you have."

Julia smiled shyly and said "Shhh" to Romeo again, with no effect whatever.

"Take him with you to the kitchen and I'll follow," Tamsin raised her voice above the yapping. And as she went in she spotted a languid teenage girl in the doorway ahead and a boy of about ten peering out through the banisters from the stairs. "Hi there!" she greeted him as she passed. The girl remained aloof, teenager-style, while the boy gave her a cheeky smile.

The children joined them in the cluttered but homely kitchen, and watched silently, the boy working his way through a packet of biscuits, as Tamsin got to work with Romeo and his embarrassed owner. It was only when Romeo - who had long since stopped barking - sat himself calmly before Tamsin in return for a tiny morsel of cheese that the lad quietly said "Wow."

The lesson went well, with both owner and dog relaxing as they worked through what Tamsin taught them. At last Julia said, "Francine, can you take Oliver and Romeo out to play football for a bit? Here, take the rest of those biscuits with you while I put the kettle on. Coffee?" she asked Tamsin, who didn't need to be asked twice. This was a golden opportunity to do some sleuthing.

"Were you checking out Major Cooper-Johnson's safari park?" asked Julia as she bustled about with the coffee things.

"It's extraordinary! Why does he have all those model animals?"

"They're field archery targets," explained Julia to Tamsin, who said "Ahhh," as everything began to slide into place.

"They put them in the bushes and undergrowth and the archers get points for where they hit them. If you look closely there are rings on them, marking where you get points."

"Sounds a bit gruesome!"

"No, it isn't really. They're only models. Much more fun than boring old targets. It just makes for a nice day out in the countryside - lots of fresh air and banter, and a few prizes thrown in at tea-time. I won this lovely arrowhead made from Tiger's Eye," she pointed to the pendant on a leather necklet round her neck. "Francine won one made of hematite - she loves it. Archery is quite skilled, you know."

"I'm sure it must be. Do you have to be very strong to shoot an arrow accurately?"

"No - it's all in the technique. Though if you were a mediaeval bowman in Olde Englande I imagine strength would have been a plus. No, both the children and I 'have a go' when there's a competition up at the Manor. All Lionel's grounds are turned over to the archers for the day."

"Exciting! Is it dangerous though, all those arrows flying about?"

"Oh, safety is very important, you're right. It's one of the first things they din into you when you start archery. They position the model animals very carefully, you see, so there's no danger of anyone being behind them. The main problem is taking ages to find your arrows when you miss and they disappear under several inches of dead leaves! Arrows are expensive, you know!"

"I suppose they would be! Tell me, this is a lovely row of cottages ..." and Tamsin didn't have the chance to ask more in the flood of Julia's response.

"It's terrible, you know. They want us all out. We've been here for years! Some of the residents were born here, *and* their parents. I'm only a blow-in, been here since Francine was small and Oliver was just a babe in arms. Lost my husband, I'm afraid."

"I'm sorry to hear that."

"Water under the bridge," she said, as she poured two mugs of coffee. "Help yourself to milk and sugar," she added, pushing them towards Tamsin, who took the milk jug and left the sugar bowl in its place. "So this place was a godsend. The rent's pretty low, you see. But I've always felt very welcome here." She gazed out of the window where she could hear Oliver shouting. "The children grew up with a dog - one of Jake's puppies, that's Jake at number 5 - a soppy old thing he was. He's buried down near the bottom of the field - not right at the bottom because of the stream that bounds all the properties," she chattered on. "So then I got Romeo. I thought his eyebrows and beard were so cute - but I didn't realise that much barking tends to come with his breed."

"Often the way with Schnauzers! But it doesn't mean we can't change it. So who else lives in this row?"

"There's the Major and his wife next to us. Then there's the Misses Damson. That's Marjorie and Edith. They were born here. They've got several cats which wind Romeo up something awful, but they're a quiet pair of old ladies. Wouldn't say boo to a goose." She looked towards the open kitchen door again as she heard Oliver playing football. Romeo had long since tired of the game and had come back in to lie in his bed at the end of the kitchen. "You can see them most days - they go out walking with their huge old-fashioned pushchair. Always dressed the same, like little girls. They collect firewood and all sorts from the hedgerows. Bats, but harmless. Then ... next to them is Pru Cunningham. She's in a nursing home at the moment, bless her, so Jake minds her chickens and keeps back the brambles in the back. He'll probably be tidying up the front again soon. I know it's got a bit scruffy. Pru would hate that."

"Poor lady. Is she likely to come out of the home?"

"We hope so. She had pneumonia, but it didn't carry her off, so she should be back. Her son Tom visits sometimes. He works in Hereford." She topped up their coffee cups, happy to have found someone to share all her gossip with. "Then the last cottage is Jake's. Salt of the earth he is. Farm labourer. And you should see his acre! It looks like a show garden. He uses every inch of it - for vegetables, fruit bushes, a small orchard where the ducks live. They can get to Pru's pond through a little doorway Jake made in the fence, you see. It's all very harmonious. He sells the things he grows, and makes a good few shillings from it."

"Maybe I'll drop in there and see what he has for sale today! I have someone coming this evening for a meal."

"There's usually a table at his gate with an honesty box. There should be some eggs and whatever's in season. His strawberries are gorgeous!"

"Mmm - must get some of them! So you have a dog. The Damson ladies have cats. Pru has chickens ... anything else?"

"Oh yes, there's Major Cooper-Johnson's pair of peacocks - that's what that meowing is that we keep hearing - and Jake has the ducks and a scrawny-looking lurcher. I mean, he looks after him alright, it's just a scrawny-looking dog. I think he probably goes poaching with the dog at night," said Julia guardedly.

"Lamping?"

"Is that what they call it? Well, let's say he augments his income where he can. He's harmless really. And everyone shops with him. So quite an asset locally. He doesn't leave his rabbits and pigeons out on public view, of course!" she laughed. "You have to ask him what he has inside."

"And all you lovely people are being threatened with eviction? That's terrible!"

"You know what's really terrible? That poor man who was killed this week. Awful business."

"I heard!" Tamsin leant forward, her elbows on the table. "Actually I'd planned to go for a walk along that path and when I got there it was swarming with police and blue lights."

"Ah, so you know about it."

"Not a lot. Who was he?" Tamsin fished brazenly.

"His name is .. *was* Roland Torben. Surveyor. He was meant to be doing some kind of geological survey of the five acres here. The Major had the idea that the watercourses underneath the land - they feed Pru's pond from the stream at the bottom, for a start - he had the idea that they could be of scientific significance and should not be ploughed up. Something to do with beetles. So he was really keen to find out what Roland might discover."

"Did he work for the developers?"

"No, that's the funny thing. You see he's been hanging around with Lionel's daughter Sara for a while. He's based in Hereford, I believe. And that's how the Major met him, on an archery shoot at the Manor. He wasn't taking part - just mooning around Sara, I think."

"Funny?"

"Oh, yes! Lionel is firmly in favour of redeveloping these cottages. I think he sees them as a bit of an eyesore, and he has tied cottages up at the Manor for his own workers, so it's not as if they're any use to him. But Sara is into the environment and ecology and all that stuff. Chalk and cheese!"

"That must cause some friction over the breakfast table?"

"So I believe. And Lionel really doesn't like - *didn't* like - Roland. Thought he wasn't good enough, you know the thing. Fathers ... As long as he's not penniless or a criminal I don't care who Francine chooses! Not my business."

"So who commissioned Roland to survey the land?"

"Nobody, I believe. I think he was just going to do it to please Sara. The Major had told him about the water-courses, and some beetle or other that relies on freshwater streams to breed. The developers must have their own surveyors. And I suppose the Council will get involved over the planning permission request."

"And someone stopped him before he could find anything out? That sounds sinister."

"Darkly sinister. Come to think of it, I remember Roland doing some surveying for the Council in the past. I wonder ..."

"You wonder if he was working for both sides?"

"Well, it's possible, isn't it?"

"And who knew which side he was working for?"

"That's a very good question ..." There was a thud on the kitchen window as Oliver's football thumped it, leaving a brown circle. "*OlivER!*" Julia adopted the universal tone of the outraged mother as she jumped up and ran to the door.

"Sorry Mum," came the boyish cry, followed by some girlish giggles from his sister.

Julia sighed as she turned back, to see Tamsin finishing her coffee and collecting her things.

"That was delicious, thank you Julia! I've enjoyed meeting Romeo and his family today. He's quite a character."

"We do love him, but it's very wearing trying to avoid everyone all the time because he barks at them. It's such a lovely area for walking, round here. I'd love it if he didn't spoil it."

"We'll get there, don't worry. Things will improve a lot. Now here's your homework till next week ..." and Tamsin handed over some sheets to her as they picked a date for their next meet-up.

As it happened, it would be the day after the public meeting.

CHAPTER SIX

Tamsin went back through the flourishing, rambling, colourful, front garden to her van, dodging some growing sunflowers and admiring the sweet peas scrambling up their supports, and as she slammed the back doors after stowing her gear there, she turned to see someone watching her.

"Good morning," she adopted her friendliest and most disarming smile.

"Morning," said the man abruptly. He was a portly gentleman, with slicked back grey hair and a large sandy-grey moustache and a rigidly erect manner. Smartly dressed in a check shirt and tailored trousers, he looked the picture of the well-heeled country gentleman. And yet he lived in a humble cottage. "Saw you looking at the animals earlier. Hmm hmm," he grunted. "Wondered if you had an interest in archery?" He raised a grey eyebrow enquiringly, his small eyes holding the characteristic fervour of an enthusiast spotting a new victim.

"I was! They're amazing. I had no idea what they were at first - I don't know anything about archery, I'm afraid."

"Come and take a look at them," he smiled, the spider beckoning her into his web.

"I'd love to!" and Tamsin stepped through the gate into his world.

"Cooper-Johnson," he said, extending his hand and grasping Tamsin's in a bruisingly firm hold. "Major, retired."

"Tamsin Kernick," she responded, extricating her squashed hand as soon as it was polite, "Dog trainer, active," she smiled.

"Ah, come to sort out young Romeo, then? Would be nice to be able to walk down the road without being barked at."

"I'll do my best. Show me your menagerie!"

And he was very happy to do so, pointing out the thin lines that marked the target areas.

"So what got you into archery," she enquired, fingering the lifelike tail feathers of the turkey.

"Something to fill the time. Arrived here. Nothing to do. Grew into rather more than a hobby. Plenty of people interested - wanted to start learning. Chose this house because of the long garden at the back. Got a target range back there. Quite safe. Got a backdrop behind it to catch any arrows that miss their mark. Let me show you!"

And Tamsin followed him as he marched down the side of his house and explained how he had started the archery craze in Bishop's Green, teaching everyone who wanted to learn, and enthusing them enough to form the Bishop's Green Archery Club. "We're always looking for new members," he added hopefully.

She could still hear the thud of Oliver kicking his football next door, and as she emerged past the house she looked in amazement at the three targets at the far end of the field - the red, white, and blue ones with the yellow bull's eye she associated with archery. They stood ranged in readiness for the next attack. Behind them was a large mesh backdrop with a few ragged holes, suspended from long poles at either end of the range. She could see the tops of the willow trees waving behind it.

"That's to stop stray arrows whacking innocent passers-by?"

"Can't be too careful. Never want anyone hurt."

"And yet someone was hurt?"

"Shocking thing. Dreadful." He shook his head so vigorously that his bushy moustache waggled. "Safety is the first thing everyone has to learn."

"But it wasn't an accident, was it?"

The Major leaned towards her and said in a low voice. "My shed was broken into last week and one recurve bow and a set of arrows taken. Didn't find out till yesterday. I keep my best bows in the house, of course. This was basic training equipment for the club. Went to get it ready for club night. Found it gone." He pursed his lips.

"So someone stole your bow and arrows?" Tamsin looked suitably horrified.

"Not only that, but because I didn't find out till after that dashed fellow got himself shot, the police don't believe me!" he fumed.

"Do you think they suspect you?"

"Who knows what they think. They aren't saying. Playing their cards close to their chest, you know. But I can tell."

"Maybe they think because you're a soldier ..."

"That I go around killing people? Nonsense! Archery is a harmless sport. Never killed anything in my life. Not with an arrow, anyway," he added, not wishing to sound as if he'd been a desk-bound soldier who saw no action.

"Wasn't it you that got the young man over here in the first place?"

"Had to do something. Not going to sit in the bunker waiting for the barbarians to arrive and destroy our homes."

"Er, quite. So how did you know him?"

"That gel Sara told me about him. Said he was into saving the environment and all that. Thought that may be a way to save the cottages. Got him interested in beetles, don't you know?"

"And you thought there's underground water here?"

"Quite so. Young fellow said he had geo-phys equipment - could x-ray the ground and see just what's down there. Extraordinary."

"Did you explain to the other cottagers what he was doing?"

"Certainly! Yes. Yes. Told 'em all. Couldn't have him just turning up in their gardens unannounced," he snorted.

A hand-bell rang in the house, and Major Cooper-Johnson jumped to attention. "There's the Mem Sahib. Must be time for Tiffin. Very pleasant to meet you m'dear." And he led her back to the side of the house.

As she bade him goodbye and started walking down the row of cottages, Tamsin marvelled at this strange caricature of a British army major - from the last century. Had he ever actually served in India? He seemed kind enough, but clearly slightly bats. Obsessed with his hobby, and convinced of its goodness. Would he want to sully his own reputation by using a bow and arrow to kill someone? And wasn't Roland Torben going to find out about protected watercourses and beetles for him? He seemed an unlikely murderer. But then, if Roland was also going to work for the other side, and perhaps not find anything of scientific interest that needed protection after all ... The Major had clearly invested a lot in his property and his club. Was it worth killing to protect?

Tamsin hadn't forgotten to visit Jake's cottage before she headed back, and she found a rickety old table in the front garden, complete with trays of various fruit and veg, some hand-scrawled notices with prices, and an honesty box. She came away with a haul of eggs, lettuce, cucumber, new potatoes, some sprigs of mint, a huge punnet of strawberries, and some gorgeous-smelling young broad beans, a firm favourite of hers and so hard to find in the shops. It all seemed to be remarkably cheap, and she looked forward to this evening's supper already. She'd seen no sign of Jake, who was presumably off labouring somewhere or in the depths of his garden at the back. It was clear that he spent a lot of time and effort nurturing his plot.

Walking back to the car, she set off on her way, giving a wave to the face she could just see in the window at no.1, past all the riotous colourful plants. Oliver was watching her go and waved back enthusiastically. She passed the fluttering police tape by the bridge and thought hard as she made her way to her next appointments - two littermates who were tearing the owner's house up, a new puppy visit, and to round off the day a deaf dog whose lovely owner needed some guidance on how to make his life just as rewarding as any dog's could be. They were carefully scheduled in a geographical grouping round Ledbury and Wellington Heath, so she could hop quickly from one to another and still have time to walk the dogs before preparing supper for her guest.

And she was eagerly looking forward to catching up with the ever-busy Feargal again!

CHAPTER SEVEN

It was fun to welcome Feargal back to Pippin Lane. He was so full of energy and enthusiasm, never still. Since they had worked together solving the Nether Trotley mystery, they had formed quite a bond and she gave him a friendly hug as he arrived through the door, noticing with interest - but no dismay - the lingering look he cast towards her much younger, and definitely lovelier, house-mate, Emerald.

"How's life on the news-hound front line?" she asked as she showed him in.

"Busy as ever!" he replied cheerily, tossing his red curls off his brow. "I'm glad you've produced something to liven my hounding - I was getting tired of cricket matches, school plays, and missing shopping trolleys."

"*I* didn't produce the murder!" protested Tamsin, offering a choice of wine or fizz to him.

He indicated the wine, "Well, let's say your unerring nose for a story placed you right on the spot again."

"That's unfortunately true. Death is beginning to follow me round."

"That sounds a bit melodramatic!" Emerald giggled. "Wrong place at the wrong time, more like."

Tamsin settled the dogs down, who were delighted to see their friend Feargal again, and gave him the full treatment of whirling tails, bright eyes, and a few soft woofs. Her shy dog Banjo had been hanging back while Quiz and Moonbeam monopolised the visitor, and her heart warmed to see Feargal take the time to give Banjo a gentle greeting.

"Let's stay in the kitchen while we put the finishing touches to dinner," she said. "Emerald, can you do your magic with the salad? I'll sort the omelettes and the broad beans. It's all Bishop's Green's finest, Feargal, fresh from the famous cottages today!"

"Sounds great. So let's hear all about it. I know you invited me to pick my brains ..."

"Brains?" echoed Emerald, with a raised eyebrow and a lopsided smile.

"Sure!" laughed Feargal, "You want me to solve this murder for you."

"Seriously though - we may need a bit of help. It's Charity, you see. She found the body, and the police seem to think this frail little old lady - who'd never been there before - shot the victim with a bow and arrows stolen from a neighbour's shed, then ditched the bow in the river."

"Now Charity is as tough as they come, but that's a bit rich?" he said. "They're surely going to pursue this one properly? They can't let mad Robin Hood wannabes roam the countryside taking potshots at people. The news desk is running this story with a vengeance. People are up in arms!"

"They are," added Emerald. "It was the talk of The Cake Stop this morning."

"Has your news desk got the whole story yet? About the five cottages?"

"I know the guy was a surveyor, and there's a planning permission pending for a plot in Bishop's Green. There's more to it?"

"Oh yes!" chorused Tamsin along with Emerald, who had finished the salad and was preparing the strawberries for afters.

So they set about detailing all the events so far for Feargal's benefit - the strange visit at Verena's, the murder, the Major, the watercourses, the theft, the Lord of the Manor's involvement, his daughter ...

"So you're saying that some disgruntled cottager or someone who thought Roland was going over to the dark side killed him? Or that the fans of the new development wanted him out of the way?"

"That's about it. Unless we can come up with something better."

"And .." Feargal went on, "that everyone in this benighted village is an expert archer? Seems pretty far-fetched."

"It's weird, isn't it. But I don't expect they're all expert. Julia and her kids, for instance. They just do it for fun."

"But they know their way round a bow and arrow," put in Emerald as she brought the dishes to the table.

"Yeah - how good do you have to be to hit something the size of a man? There were quite a few arrows that missed, and were stuck in the ground, you tell me?" Feargal turned to Tamsin.

"If arrows were raining down on him, presumably the guy was moving - fast. Maybe the mystery archer is used to static targets, like the animals I saw, or those round coloured targets .."

"Or maybe they were perfectly able to hit their stationary victim with the first arrow, then fired a few around to make it look like they weren't very good at it."

Feargal smiled at Emerald admiringly. "Emerald! That is brilliant! You always take a fresh look at things," he added. "You have a way of seeing things differently."

"Oh, thanks. Just seemed obvious to me ..."

Tamsin smiled at this interaction and said, "That's why we need you in on this! Your shafts of insight are blisteringly important! So perhaps we're looking for someone who's good at archery, as well as wanting Roland off the scene."

"I used to do a bit of target archery back in Brum, maybe I should go along to the club night and join and see what I can learn," Feargal chipped in.

"That's a great idea! Were you any good?"

"Mmm - mediocre, I'd say. I fancied a super-posh compound bow, super-expensive too. But they'd only let the youngsters use recurves."

Emerald shook her head in bafflement.

"Basically ancient versus modern. The compound bows are like machines, made of carbon fibre, metal, and whatnot. The recurves are more traditional, mostly wooden. You can guess which one a teenage boy lusted after!"

"It was a recurve that was stolen from the Major's shed," said Tamsin thoughtfully. "He talked of Club Night, so presumably it happens every week. I think maybe today, Friday," she thought back to what he'd said about the break-in.

Emerald put down her fork, swallowing her mouthful with relish. "Hey these eggs are delicious! So yellow too ..."

"I'm enjoying the broad beans - haven't had them since I was a kid." Feargal munched happily.

"There's nothing like proper home-grown food," said Tamsin, helping herself to some more new potatoes. It's awful to think that amazing garden of Jake's could get wrecked by diggers and people wanting to commute and pretend to live in the country, when the people who are actually doing it right will get displaced. You could see just how much care he lavishes on his patch."

"Throwing people off their land is bad. I'm always sorry for the Irish - how they were dispossessed by their English masters."

"Perhaps you *have* got Irish blood after all?" Emerald eyed him and his red hair thoughtfully.

"Maybe!" he smiled. "Or maybe my mother was frightened by a leprechaun when she was expecting me! But it *is* wrong. And you tell me those people have been there for donkey's years?"

"Yes, some were born there. And they really do use their acres. They all seem to be growing food, or keeping hens, or something."

"Except for the mad Major?"

"True. I didn't see any veg patch there - but he's certainly using his acre too, and benefitting his neighbours by running the club there."

"Not one of them," Emerald rose to clear the plates.

"True. But I don't know if Torben was a neighbour. I don't know where he actually lived. I know he had a bit of a thing going with Lionel's daughter over at the Manor. So perhaps he was often around. I keep thinking of when he burst into Mike and Verena's place. Should we have done something? Perhaps his killer was on his tail then. We *should* have done something!"

"You can't blame yourself, old thing," Feargal soothed her. "From what you say it all happened very fast, and Mike did look out after him."

They fell to eating the strawberries, whose scent was irresistible.

"When are you back in Bishop's Green?" asked Emerald. "I could give you a shopping list!"

"You can be sure I'll be stopping off at Jake's again. These are simply gorgeous - so much better than what you can get in the shops."

"I'll be over there too, when I go to the Archery Club." Feargal polished off the last of his strawberries and cream.

"I'm dying to hear what you find out!"

"But there's something else we have to go to first, isn't there?" Emerald put in.

"Yes! The famous meeting! That's going to be on Thursday. You coming, Feargal?"

"You bet! Know what, I'll barely know you two -"

"Three - Charity's coming too."

"Three. I may learn more if I'm on my own."

"Right-o. We'll hit them on two fronts. I'm super practical. Charity's very good at being fluffy. And Emerald ... you just captivate people. We can all split up and see what we can find out."

"I'm not just a pretty face, you know," objected Emerald. "I love a bit of aggro!"

Tamsin looked at her ethereal friend and shook her head, smiling. "Then you'll have to meet Verena. She's beside herself with excitement at this turmoil in their little backwater."

"You know," said Feargal, "this meal has given me renewed energy for the fray. Not just that I'm now full to the gunwales - for which many thanks - but the thought of these people being thrown off their land. It's awful. I'll see what we can generate by way of a campaign on the paper."

"It has plenty of publicity already with poor Roland getting skewered."

"We can solve that crime at the same time as rescuing the cottages! *Thunderbirds are go!*"

The dogs pricked up their ears at the sound of the laughter, and sure enough they were rewarded with strawberry hulls being tossed out for them each to catch, one by one.

CHAPTER EIGHT

After her Saturday morning classes in Malvern the next day, Tamsin grabbed lunch at The Cake Stop before heading off for her afternoon calls.

"I see *Mademoiselle* Quiz has honoured us with a *visite* today," said Jean-Philippe as he prepared her coffee and he slipped the dog a bit of broken biscuit.

"She's been working today! Showing the Tricks Class how to do 'Bang, you're dead!'"

"Intriguing! You shoot your dog?"

Tamsin laughed as she took the coffee and toasted sandwich. "I point two fingers at her - you know, like a gun - and say *Bang!* ..." Hearing her cue, Quiz hurled herself flat on her side and remained motionless, to the consternation of the lady who was next in the queue.

"Oops, sorry! She loves to show off!" Tamsin reassured the lady, who laughed and patted her chest with relief.

"As do you!" said Jean-Philippe as he raised one of his bushy black eyebrows.

"Got a minute?" she said, as she turned to look for a table.

"Sure - *un moment.* Now *Madame,* what can I give you?" he turned to the next customer, "Apart from an assurance that there will be no more dead dogs at your feet!"

When Jean-Philippe got the chance to wander over to Tamsin's table, she was busy making lists.

"You've heard of this Robin Hood Murder, as the papers are calling it?" Her face softened as she saw Jean-Philippe fondle Quiz's ears. "How did you know she likes that? Some dogs hate their ears being touched."

"Trial and error, I guess. Her chin is pressed into my knee, so I'm assuming she wants me to continue a bit longer. And yes, I've heard about the murder. You're not involved are you? *Encore? Mon Dieu!*"

"Not exactly ... well yes, sort of. You see Charity was meeting me for a walk there and she discovered the body. The police took her in for questioning - it was awful."

"I'd heard that. But I was glad to see her walking by the cafe with her *petite chienne* earlier today. I didn't know you were behind it, though."

"Not by choice, I can assure you! I'm training some of the village dogs over there now. I started with one and she recommended me to a couple of others. So I'm getting to know a bit about what's going on below the surface of this tranquil Herefordshire hamlet."

"And you can't resist having a go at outwitting the police again?" the Barista gave her a knowing look.

"No!" Tamsin looked down at Quiz. "Yes .. You're right, I can't resist. It's fascinating, and I was there just after the police. I saw the body." She paused for a moment at the enormity of the crime, and stroked Quiz's head which had been transferred to her own knee. "I'm making a list right now, of who and what and why." She turned the list to face him. "There's a lot I don't know, and I wondered ... I know it's rather off your patch ..."

"It is. Most people from that side of Malvern would do their shopping in Hereford. But I tell you what: I can ask Jeremy. He runs that coffee shop in the Old Market centre in Hereford. Always good for a gossip, is Jeremy!"

"Goodness! There's a coffee shop underground network?"

"We keep in touch," he smiled, and looked back to the counter where the queue was growing. "I need to help Kylie."

"Let me know what you find out!"

"*Bien sûr!* For sure I will."

Tamsin cast an eye at the clock on the wall - a curious clock with all the numbers in a jumble at the bottom and the hands pointing at empty space, reminding her of how hard it had been to learn to tell the time as a child. She stashed her notebook in her bag, gathered up Quiz's mat, asked the dog to pick up her lead and give it to her, and set off. "We've got some visits to make, Quiz!"

And it was with relief after a particularly difficult visit out in the sticks with someone who felt they had to shout at their dog "to show him who's boss", but who grudgingly agreed to try just one of her ideas, that she decided it was time to clear her head with a bit of fresh air.

She passed a sign for Bingham Parva and thought of the orchard her clients-cum-friends - so many of them became friends - Maggie and Don had sent her to. "It's not far away, Quizzy, let's go and relax. You've had a good sleep."

And as she pulled to the side of the road and unloaded her dog, she spotted someone approaching, with a big black Labrador.

"Talk of the devil! Hi Maggie, hello Jez! You just going?"

"Hello! And hello Quiz - I'm good for another circuit. Want some company?"

"That would be lovely," and the two friends released their friendly dogs to snuffle around together and set off along the avenues between the rows of apple trees.

"That's one of the reasons we wanted an older dog," Maggie indicated the two big dogs peaceably walking together. "Calmer, less scatty than a puppy."

"You struck lucky with Jez. Sometimes rehomed dogs come with a boatload of problems."

"We're lucky that Jez is a typical Lab - do anything for a biscuit! You been visiting a client round here?"

Tamsin told her a little about her challenging visit - without mentioning any names.

"He'll come round," Maggie assured her. "Once he sees how easily your magic works!"

"Hope so."

"And I hear from Don that you were on the spot for our little local excitement."

"Afraid I was. I'd arranged to meet Charity there for a walk - such a lovely spot - you remember Charity from our walk?"

"Yes, lovely old lady. Steel wrapped in fluff."

"Well said! Yes, she's a tough old bird - but she was very upset by the police hauling her in."

"Procedure. They're so closely watched these days - they don't want to get caught out for missing steps. There have been tragic consequences ..."

"But you'd think they could unbend a little. Charity hardly presents as a master criminal."

"True," Maggie laughed. "Anyhow the victim ended up on my slab, so they won't be troubling her any more."

Tamsin stopped and looked at Maggie hopefully. "Time of death rules her out?"

"Time of death definitely rules her out. I gather they have footage of her driving out of Malvern that morning and they can fix the time. I can't tell you very much." As a pathologist working for the police, Maggie had to keep most information to herself. "But I can divulge that anyone patrolling the riverbank with a bow and arrow earlier in the morning could find themselves brought in for questioning."

"Nothing more precise than that?"

"Not at the moment."

"That gives me something to go on."

"You're investigating! 'Tamsin the Malvern Hills Detective' rides again?"

"Well, I seem to be all tangled up in it. And I do feel for those cottagers. I've no idea if any of them did it - or if there are other forces at work. But I'm going along to their meeting next week. Just to show solidarity with tradition, I suppose."

"I thought I may wander along too. Don's interested because a lot of the residents of Bishop's Green would be his patients. It helps to know what's going on in their lives if they turn up in the surgery next week with high blood pressure."

"Or arrow wounds!" laughed Tamsin.

"Let's hope feelings aren't running so high that there'll be a repetition."

"So you think it's connected?"

"A surveyor involved in an unpopular development gets killed? Got to be more than a coincidence, don't you think?"

"Unless that's a smokescreen. Someone taking advantage of the situation to hide their crime ... like a discarded lover getting killed then hidden in a bombed house in the war - I read a book about that not long ago."

"You have a fiery imagination!" said Maggie, calling Jez over to put his lead on, as they had reached the entrance again.

"I think there could be more to it than meets the eye. Just got a feeling. I'm going to the Manor House at Bishop's Green on Monday," she turned to address Jez, "to meet another soppy Labrador! And they're bound to have some thoughts to offer on their local *cause célèbre*."

"You can check whether they're early risers!" laughed Maggie, as she headed away with her dog.

CHAPTER NINE

Tamsin drove through the splendid gateway to the Manor House on a glorious sunny Monday morning. The drive wound through undulating parkland and mature trees. Sheep grazed the unfenced pastures, and she had to slow down a couple of times to allow some ewes and their lambs to raise themselves from the sun-warmed tarmac and shuffle aside for her to pass - at least, the ewes shuffled and the lambs bounced and pranced! At last she reached a cattle grid signalling the extent of the sheep's freedom. The dip of the steep ha-ha prevented the sheep from invading the Manor gardens while permitting an open view from the large south-facing windows of the house, uncluttered with fencing. A ha-ha is like a modern infinity pool, she thought: there's nothing new under the sun!

Pulling up at the door, she realised this Manor House was more like a stately home in its appearance. Though not huge, it certainly imparted a feeling of wealth and power. The large door had an oversized old-fashioned bell-pull beside it. She pulled it with no little trepidation, and heard a jangling in the depths of the house within, followed by some deep barks.

When the door opened, the source of the barks ran towards her with excitement.

"Grouse!" called his owner, "Get in!"

But this had little effect and Grouse would have thumped Tamsin right in the breadbasket if she hadn't foreseen this and dodged at the last moment, while the lollopy dog continued to greet her with fervour. She pulled out some treats from her pocket and got a sit, a drool, and a down in quick succession. "He's ok," she said, to stop his owner yelling at him, "Come on Grouse!" and she stepped towards the door.

"You've discovered the way to his heart already - it's directly connected to his stomach," said Lionel tersely as he led the way through the vast dark hallway to a large study, equipped with armchairs as well as a desk sporting all the computer gear associated with a modern business. He motioned Tamsin to a chair and parked himself in a swivel chair which suited his energetic character and need to be moving. Tamsin started to feel sea-sick as he swivelled back and forth. "But I don't hold with bribing a dog," he warned, "he's a working dog - needs to do what he's told."

"Well .. you have to feed him anyway, so you may as well get some mileage out of it!" countered Tamsin, so familiar by now with this strange attitude - that a dog was not a sentient being but a machine that needed basic fuel and should then run correctly without further input.

"I need him to listen and not run off. That's all."

"He lives in the house with you?"

"I like to have a dog around. Always have done. It's just that this one seems a bit of a handful."

"That gives us a great start - he'll want to please you: it's just a question of showing him how."

So the session went smoothly on, with Tamsin agreeing with everything Lionel said, then teaching him to do the exact opposite so he got the results he wanted. At one stage the door opened and a slim girl wearing sports gear, her long dark hair swinging in a pony tail, came in. "Can I print something Dad?" she asked.

"Certainly my dear. More Save the Whale posters? This is my daughter Sara - Sara, meet er .. Tamsin Kernick. She's come to knock some sense into Grouse's bone head." Sara nodded with little interest and said "Hello Tamsin," obediently, and "good luck with that!" as she scanned her document into the printer.

So this was the object of Roland Torben's affections, thought Tamsin. She was a nice enough looking girl, about eighteen, she thought.

And as Sara took the pages she'd printed, she added, "Mum says there's coffee in the kitchen if you would like some," gave a quick smile and left the room.

"Good plan - you can meet Felicity and see where Grouse sleeps. You were asking about his sleeping arrangements, weren't you?"

So they set off back down the huge gloomy hallway, along a tiled corridor and through a large dark wooden door. Into a kitchen straight out of a glossy magazine. It was large, light, modern, and comfortable. There was a very large scrubbed deal table surrounded by wheelback chairs, the ones at each end of the table with arms, and a top-of-the-range Aga, of a size suited to cook for an army. On the table were a cafetière, several mugs which Tamsin recognised as the work of one of the more expensive potters in the area, and a big cream jug.

"Hello, you must be Tamsin!" Felicity greeted her effusively. She appeared the typical Lady of the Manor, slim, with expensively cut trousers, pale pink cashmere cardigan, and masses of auburn curls falling over her shoulders. "Been teaching the thick mutt some new tricks?"

No wonder Grouse behaved as he did, thought Tamsin. They all have such a low opinion of him.

"He's a lovely dog," she countered, "I look forward to teaching him loads!"

"This is where he sleeps," said Lionel, pointing to a large bed up against the side of the Aga. He still looked puzzled at her interest in this aspect of Grouse's life.

"Looks perfect," Tamsin smiled as she took the offered chair and mug of coffee. "I hadn't realised quite how big your home was."

"It's enormous," said Felicity. "Built when it was normal to have a fleet of servants to run it. We've had to make lots of changes to fit in with how people live these days. Central heating, for a start. You'd need a constant stream of parlourmaids with coal buckets to keep all the fires burning in all the downstairs rooms, never mind the bedrooms too."

Tamsin nodded appreciatively. "So you don't have staff at all now?"

"There's a cleaner, that's all. And the Estate Manager of course. Gamekeepers, that kind of thing. The Estate Manager manages the formal gardens too, though I call the shots there and look after the flowers. The heathens would think them all weeds and pull 'em out without a backward glance. I learnt my lesson when a clump of cowslips I was nurturing disappeared. 'Thought they was dandelions,' was the response I got."

"The place costs a fortune to keep upright," Lionel said ruefully. "It started off as the Bishop's summer property, you know. He had the Palace in the city that went with his office, and had this place on the side. Pretty wealthy in those days, the Church. And a lot of the land was sold off to pay gambling debts a couple of hundred years ago. The farm is too small to support it any more. So we run shoots and other events to keep the cash flowing. We do weddings as well, in the Great Barn. And we're planning to make the stable block into a conference centre."

"How very enterprising! I guess we all have to accommodate change. I remember reading about your wedding venue in a magazine."

"Oh, do you take *Our County Matters*?" asked Felicity with interest.

"Er, no. Think it was at the dentist's actually!" Tamsin looked abashed, laughed, and went on, "But some change is so good! My bookings all had to be done by post when I started out. So easy now, with the interwebs and all that," she smiled as she sipped her coffee. "And yes, you run the Field Archery Competition, don't you?" asked Tamsin, keen to move this conversation to what she was really interested in finding out.

"We do. The woodland on the hilly parts of the estate lends itself to that kind of thing well."

"You're not going to go ahead with it this year are you, Daddy?" Sara had entered the room through a door behind Tamsin. "Not after .. what happened to Roland!"

"It's not until the Autumn. Everyone will have forgotten by then." Lionel cast a look at his daughter to see how this was met. And to

Tamsin's surprise, Sara shrugged and poured herself a mug of coffee, taking it to the window where she gazed at the view of the woods on the hills beyond, before slumping into the window seat.

"You knew the ... the unfortunate man? I'm so sorry," said Tamsin.

"We hung out sometimes. I liked him," she said defiantly.

"We all met him," said Felicity. "He was a surveyor from Hereford. He specialised in environmental projects and it seems he had been commissioned to produce a survey on the land behind the cottages on the road in to Bishop's Green. Know them?"

"Er, yes, I think I know the cottages you mean."

Lionel butted in: "They want to develop it. Get rid of those eyesores and build some decent houses. Good idea. It would bring in the sort of people we need to use our facilities."

"But I think I heard this surveyor was checking out the environmental impact? So he wasn't working for the developers?"

"No. One of the cottagers appointed him I believe. Hoping that some rare water-beetle or something would stop the project in its tracks. Ridiculous." Lionel snorted contemptuously.

"You make it sound as if you don't care for the environment, darling," interjected Felicity. "You do a lot to preserve the landscape."

"It works well for the shoots. But you can't stand in the way of progress."

"Are you suggesting someone did away with the poor fellow to stop him finding water-beetles?" Tamsin asked tentatively.

Felicity jumped in with her answer before Lionel could open his mouth, "No-one round here would do something like that! It must have been an accident. Someone fooling about with a bow and arrow and Roland just got in the way."

"I hope you're right. But I imagine feelings are running high over the cottage proposal. Tends to be the way in country places," Tamsin responded. "There was some proposal for a development near an old tin-mine in Cornwall - my cousin lives down there. All hell was let loose! Quiet old biddies who normally wouldn't say boo to a goose were up in arms, campaigning alongside their teenage grandchildren!"

Lionel spoke: "People don't like change. But land-owners have to do their best to get a return on their investment. We're not charities!"

"What's going to happen to the people who live there, if the plan goes ahead?"

"*When* it goes ahead. It'll happen, you mark my words."

Felicity tried a softer tone. "They're all renting. If there were ever any leases they're long out of date, so they just live month to month. They always knew they had no security of tenure."

"They'll have to get to grips with real life and find themselves somewhere else to live," said Lionel huffily.

Sara sighed loudly and rose from the window seat, "I'll be glad when I get to Uni and can stop hearing about these piddling local issues." She raised her voice as she addressed her father. "Roland had it right, investigating water-beetles. Everything's connected. And anything that threatens water-beetles threatens the environment. The world is on fire! Don't you get it?" She banged her mug down by the sink and swept from the room.

"She's still upset about Roland," said Felicity quietly, trying to explain away her daughter's lapse in manners.

"Did you know him well?" said Tamsin, absently stroking the big head of Grouse that was resting heavily on her leg.

"We knew enough. Seems he had a woman in tow already. Not suitable for Sara at all." Lionel put in grumpily, while Felicity eyed him with a worried expression.

"Oh. Like that, was he? Hmm, I didn't have him down as a philanderer!"

"You knew him?" asked Felicity sharply.

"No. I didn't know him - but I, er, ran into him once. He seemed a shy fellow."

"Well, we're rid of him now." Lionel stood up. "Got to go and see Jackson."

"Jackson's the Estate Manager," said Felicity. "Vital cog in the machine!"

Tamsin took her cue and whipped out her diary to confirm their next date. "Here are some notes on what we did today. Do you think you can spend two minutes a day on this one," she pointed on the page, "and another three on that one?"

"I'll try. Busy, you know."

"Of course. Perhaps you could do the first one just before your morning walk round the estate with Grouse - and the other one .. maybe just before supper?"

"That's a good idea, darling," Felicity was ready to smooth the path with her husband again, as seemed to be her constant task. "I'll remind you!" she added brightly.

After effusive thanks for the coffee, Tamsin bade them all - including Grouse - a fond goodbye, and drove back through the sheep pasture to the outside world, dodging bleating lambs as they ran to catch up with their ambling mothers. It certainly felt like another world she'd visited for the morning. "They do things differently there," she thought.

CHAPTER TEN

"There's spinach, more strawberries, and gossip, for supper!" Tamsin said as the dogs rushed towards the door to greet Emerald, just returning from one of her yoga classes.

"Fantastic!" said Emerald, dropping her yoga bag by the stairs and coming to inspect the food preparation, wading through the dogs. "Yes, hallo all of you. Yes, lovely to see you again. Yes, me too," she chattered as she scooped up Opal from the worktop and snuggled her fondly.

"Tired?"

"Yes. Just did two privates and a class at The Cake Stop. Whacked!"

"How's Jean-Philippe?"

"He's full of the murder. Didn't get a chance to talk to him as the Furies were delivering a load of gorgeous-looking cakes. He says he's got something to tell you, but it'll keep till tomorrow."

"Fascinating! That gives me an excuse to sample some of that cake."

"That was probably his plan," laughed Emerald, swiping a strawberry, and lifting a saucepan lid and peering in through the steam. "Ooh, new potatoes and mint too! What a treat. I take it you've been to Bishop's Green to forage for goodies?"

"Yes. Met the Lord of the Manor today. Funny lot of people. It's a different life they lead, with all that wealth behind them. Gives them a different view of the world."

"I'm sure there are some very good and generous land-owners." Emerald was always quick to offer a balancing view.

"True enough. But Lionel's attitude kinda grated with me. He sees the cottagers as commodities, not people. I get that landlords need to turn a profit. Just like you and me. But it seemed callous somehow. It's not as if they're his cottages."

"Bet you're glad you own your own house!"

Tamsin laughed loudly, "The bank owns my house! But I know what you mean."

They feasted on all the fresh food till all that was left was a sprig of mint and some strawberry hulls - for which the dogs waited patiently while Opal the cat looked on in bafflement, seeing them eating what was clearly quite inedible. Then Tamsin said, "What was weird was the tension in that household. Lionel's, I mean. Seems the daughter, Sara, was going out with Roland. Though she doesn't look all that upset about his demise. But here's the thing," she leant forward, elbows on the table, "Lionel seemed to think Roland already had a woman 'in tow', as he put it. Maybe he was being the heavy father and protecting Sara?"

"Seems a bit drastic. Thought you said Torben was like a frightened rabbit? Doesn't sound like a leching Lothario!"

"He certainly doesn't. But I think Lionel said that for a reason. I mean, it seems to have importance somehow."

"Well *I* think it's all to do with the cottages. And I'm expecting fire-works on Thursday night! I'll be very disappointed if there aren't any."

"Be careful what you wish for!"

As they cleared away, Tamsin went to run through her phone messages and deal with her enquiries. "Oh, Feargal's left a message," she said, switching it to loudspeaker.

"Just thought I'd tell you - the paper's started the campaign! Take a look at the web edition. See you Thursday."

Emerald snatched up her phone and scrolled quickly to the page. "Look! Photos of the cottages - this is your strawberry-grower, isn't it?"

She showed Tamsin the screen, with a photo of a grim-faced, nut-brown, middle-aged man with a rake in hand.

"Must be. I haven't met him yet. What else do they have?"

"Plans to evict cottagers are dividing village," she read out. "Ooh, they're ramping it up alright. They're enlisting support at the meeting on Thursday ... requests to keep calm ... already been one death - feelings running high ..."

"They actually say the death is because of the plans?"

"N-n-no," Emerald scanned the page quickly. "But it's implied. And it *is* connected. Got to be."

"I had a thought - when I ran into Maggie on Saturday - you know, the police pathologist? With Jez?" Emerald nodded. "I was talking to her of a book I read where a house was bombed during the war, and one of the bodies had a knife stuck in it. Seems it had been put there after the bombing and before the house collapsed."

"Ooh yes. That's like when they were excavating a plague pit from the 1600s a few years back, in London. One of the skeletons had a hole in its head. Very fishy ... So you think someone's using this cottage business to cover up a simple murder?"

"Could be. Think Miss Marple! Didn't she say the solution lay in understanding the victim - or was it some other fictional detective?"

"You mean, not a real one, like you?" Emerald giggled.

"*Anyway,*" Tamsin smirked back, "it's a question of finding out why anyone would want him dead. The police have all the evidence, the forensics and all that. We have to soldier on without that - we just use the little grey cells, *oui?* Though we do know now that he was killed early in the morning."

"Oh yes, I'd forgotten that. What did Charity say when you told her? I guess you did tell her?"

"Of course! I was on the blower to her as soon as I got home. She's relieved, but still won't feel happy till they've got the right person. Better get on with these messages ..."

And after returning a few calls and making some class bookings, she chucked down her pen, sighed ... and the phone rang again.

She scooped it up and barely had time to answer before Julia jumped in with a question about what she should do with Romeo when he wasn't interested in doing anything except barking. Tamsin listened patiently, then asked her how she was doing with the homework she'd set.

"Oh, I'm doing that - every day!" Julia replied like a good schoolgirl. "And it is helping. Yes, it's definitely helping ..."

"Then you'll need to keep doing it - I have a lot more to give you. We'll make a start on Friday."

"I'll be looking forward to seeing you, but I think we may still be nursing bruises from the night before .." she giggled.

"You expecting the meeting to get rough?"

"Tempers are definitely getting frayed round here. You know," she went on in a confidential voice, "Pru's son Tom was here today, and there was the most awful hullabaloo."

This is why she rang me, Tamsin thought to herself - she couldn't wait to tell someone!

"That's Pru from number ... ?"

"No.4. Pru's still in the home, poor love, but Tom drops in to keep the front tidy and check on things. And he had a *huge* row with Jake today," she sounded triumphant.

"Didn't you say Jake was looking after Pru's chickens?"

"Yes, he is. And I'm sure Tom's happy about that. Jake gets paid in eggs, you see. But Tom has a plumbing business over in Hereford!"

Tamsin waited patiently, failing to see the connection.

"He wants the plumbing contract on the new development!" explained Julia to her dim audience.

"Oh, so he's the one cottager who's in favour of the plan?"

"*Tom* is. But Pru's not, of course. She's hoping to be back at home as soon as she's recovered and she can get about ok."

"And Jake didn't take kindly to Tom's ideas?"

"He did not! It's all rather worrying really. As that meeting gets closer it becomes more real. I so hope we won't have to leave .."

"I hope you won't too, Julia. I'm fascinated by this meeting. I've been invited along, so I'll see you there. I hope I don't have to bring a hard hat!"

She ended the call and went into the living room where Emerald was listening to some New Age kind of music, stretched out on the sofa with a soporific cat on her tummy.

Emerald opened one eye and said with a smile, "Looks as though this meeting will be a sell-out!"

<h1 style="text-align:center">CHAPTER ELEVEN</h1>

Tamsin was pleased to have a reason to visit The Cake Stop the next morning. And she'd skipped breakfast so she could justify cake.

The Furies had excelled themselves, and she went straight for the passionfruit meringue. It had a hint of lemon, and mango curd, and it was mouthwateringly good.

"Here you go, Moonbeam." She sat with Moonbeam on her lap and put a dot of cream from her finger on the end of the little dog's nose, laughing at her going cross-eyed in her antics to lick it off.

Kylie - Jean-Philippe's trainee barista, was happily chattering to the customers as she served them, tossing her pink hair back as she laughed. So the man himself was free to stroll over to join Tamsin.

"I spoke to Jeremy," he said as he sat down opposite her. "This is Moonbeam, right?" He addressed the little dog politely and was greeted with a furiously wagging pointy tail. Another dot of cream on her nose settled her again.

"And?"

"He knew exactly who I meant. Seems your Roland used his cafe as a meeting place with Sara. Jeremy didn't seem to think there was much chemistry between them, but they shared a passion for environmental issues. She's always organising 'peaceful protests' and sticking posters up all over the place."

Tamsin remembered the posters she saw Sara print in her father's office, and nodded encouragingly.

"So they were pretending to go out together, when in fact they were plotting unrest and using that as a cover?"

"That seems to sum it up."

"Lionel said Roland had a woman already. That figures, if Sara was not a girlfriend."

"*C'est vrai.*"

Tamsin gave Moonbeam another lick of cream as she took a drink of her coffee. "How come your coffee always tastes divine?"

"It's my magic touch," smiled Jean-Philippe. "There's more, you know."

"Go on."

"Jeremy had the impression they wanted to use the cottage survey to get a new protest going. A few of their rent-a-crowd fellow protesters would meet with them sometimes. They would get quite noisy in their enthusiasm."

"So there's a gang of these people, getting ready to make a big thing out of this development? Hmm .." She stroked Moonbeam thoughtfully. "Maybe that made it important for someone to stop them."

"*Mais*, did everyone know whose side Torben was on?"

"Oh, you mean one of the cottagers may have thought he was from the developers?"

"Well, it's possible, isn't it? If they just saw him snooping about in his suit, measuring things with that contraption they use .."

"A theodolite."

"Yeah, one of them," he smiled.

"Major Cooper-Johnson had told him about the water-courses. But I suppose he may still have thought he was representing the developers and was just trying to put his oar in. I can't believe Julia could kill anyone, though she really, really doesn't want to lose her cottage." She put down her mug to count the cottagers on her fingers. "Pru

Cunningham is recuperating from an illness in a nursing home, but her son Tom is very much pro the building work - he's a plumber and he wants in on the contract. Jake the market gardener is obviously completely against - his garden must have taken donkey's years to get it to its present super-productive state - and he may not have known anything about Sara's involvement. He doesn't work at the Manor at all as far as I can tell."

"Is that all of them?"

"There's the Misses Damson at no.3 as well. Lots of cats. But they"re ancient. Could they really have taken matters into their own hands?"

"They may have the most to lose. They may think themselves too old to start again."

"You're right. I think I need to visit them. I'll see if I can think up a cat-related excuse ..."

"Tamsin is on the case!" Jean-Philippe mocked.

"It's harder this time, actually," she chose to ignore the mockery. "I can't ask them where they were at the time. I could do that with - you know - the Nether Trotley business, as it was my class they were at. But I'm just an outsider here."

"*Si*, but you solved the case by understanding the people involved! The police had all the evidence and timings and alibis and whatnot. You did it through .. inspiration!" Jean-Philippe waved his arm in the air dramatically.

"You're right. I was just piecing some things together that didn't fit. Talking to the suspects - seems funny to call my students suspects - but it let these things emerge. The things that didn't make sense. And I'm already learning a lot now that doesn't make sense!"

"You'll get there! Keep talking to them - that's quite a gift you have, must go alongside being able to talk to animals," he winked at Moonbeam, "and it'll start to fall into place."

"Or not!"

"Take care *mon amie*. Whoever did that dreadful thing is either hard of heart or mentally on the run. They could do it again. Don't put your life in danger." He stood up and draped his tea-towel over his shoulder with a flourish. "I'd never get through all this cake! I'd have to reduce the Furies' order!" he laughed.

"No chance! I'd come back and haunt you, and eat all the cakes in the night," Tamsin laughed in return. But she valued her friend's concern, and she knew he was right. "I'll take care, promise."

She returned to her interrupted meringue, and was just polishing it off when into the cafe came Charity, explaining happily to Muffin where they were.

"Hello, my dear," she called across the room as she approached, nodding and smiling to the other visitors with ever a friendly word or two, as she wound her way through the chairs, Muffin pulling ahead of her on her lead.

It took her a while to reach Tamsin, as people smiled and chatted back as she passed. "She knows everyone," thought Tamsin, "and they all love her."

Muffin was straining to reach Tamsin and Moonbeam, threatening to knock over chairs and trip Kylie up, so Tamsin called out, "Let go of her, Charity," and Muffin shot like a bullet to her as if she hadn't seen her for weeks. She gathered up her trailing lead and kept her amused till Charity's royal progress was complete and she arrived at the armchair Jean-Philippe had just vacated.

"Well, have you heard the latest?" she said without preamble.

"No? What's happened?"

"It was in the *Mercury* online this morning. Your friend Verena has been talking to Feargal. There's a picture of her holding her puppy - have a look - you're quicker at getting round these gadgets than I am. It's just after the *Save the Cottages Campaign* pictures ..."

Tamsin obediently started searching on her phone, and soon came up with the photo in question. "Aww, that's Bingo! Such a poppet ..." Her face softened as she tilted her head to gaze enraptured at the puppy's picture.

"Bother Bingo! Look at what Verena said!" said Charity with impatience.

"We saw Mr.Torben a couple of days before the tragedy." Tamsin read

out, *"He seemed to be running from someone. No, we didn't see who, but he was really frightened! Of course, we had no idea who he was at the time. Thought he was some kind of escaped nut!"*

"Isn't that what happened when you were there, Tamsin?"

"Yes, that's right. It was weird alright. Mike followed him out and looked about but saw nothing. Perhaps he was being chased by a mad archer then?"

"I imagine Inspector Hawkins will want to learn more about this."

"*Chief* Inspector Hawkins, if you don't mind," smiled Tamsin.

"Whatever. They'll probably wonder why they weren't told earlier. You're not going to get into trouble are you, dear?"

"Oh Lord, I hope not. I was just a visitor in their home at the time. Didn't feel it was anything to do with me. How wrong can a girl be?"

"Ooh - before I forget! - I have to show you ... look at this, Tamsin!" Charity stood up again and held her arm out towards Muffin, who grabbed the sleeve obligingly.

"That's a great start! She's a fast learner. Next you want her to start pulling. You may go back to your cloth to teach that, a bit like Tug."

"This is such fun! When do I add the word? What word should I use?"

Tamsin frowned. "Do you use the word 'pull' for anything?"

"'Pull'? No, I don't."

"I'd use Pull then. Once she's got Pull you can use it for all sorts of things. I'd struggle to change my duvet cover without Quiz hanging on to it while I pull the duvet out."

"Oh, how useful!" Kylie approached with Charity's favoured cup of tea. "Oh thank you, Kylie! I'll be over in a moment to settle up. How thoughtful of you."

Kylie flicked back her pink hair and smiled broadly, "We look after our special customers, Charity!"

"Now, that makes me think," Tamsin went on as Kylie departed, swishing her tiny multi-coloured ra-ra skirt as she spun round. "If Roland was in fear of his life on Tuesday, when I went round to Verena's, he would surely have told his environmentalist mates, wouldn't he? That was the connection, apparently - he was part of a cell of protesters, along with Sara. They let her parents think she was going out with him, rather than see that she was involved with the protest campaign. Perhaps I should catch Sara on her own, away from her father. Maybe she'll let on what she knows. They can't like one of their number being scythed down, even if they weren't romantically involved."

"You're right, I'm sure."

Tamsin waved her hand and mouthed "Jean-Philippe" when he looked in her direction, and motioned him to come over. Explaining what she'd just been thinking, she asked if he could have another word with Jeremy and find out more about who these friends were. "If we knew where they can be found, when they meet, that could be another lead to follow."

"Your wish is my command, *Mademoiselle*," he said, clicking his heels together.

"That looks more Prussian than French," she giggled.

He relapsed into his usual voice and said, "I'll do my best," before placing a hand on each dog's head - both of them perched on their people's laps - and going back to his duties.

CHAPTER TWELVE

After an early visit to the several Malvern vets to re-stock their supply of Top Dogs flyers, and a quick catch-up chat with the receptionists, Tamsin found herself in Verena and Mike's kitchen again. Bingo was awake for the whole session this time, and she delighted in his bright eyes and waving tail as he learnt everything he could as fast as possible. "He's like a sponge!" she told them, enthusiastically, "the way he soaks everything up!"

And when they were seated round the kitchen table with the customary cafetière of coffee - This is a great village for good coffee, thought Tamsin - they went back to the subject at the front of their minds.

"I see the *Malvern Mercury* tracked you down?" she offered.

Mike scowled as Verena said, "I didn't know who they were - just thought they were from a neighbouring village, wanting a gossip. Mike is really cross with me ..."

"Well, you told no lies. That's what happened alright."

"You're right! And now I know who these vultures are, I'm keeping myself to myself," she looked to Mike for approval.

"Actually, I've met their reporter Feargal - red-headed guy - is that who it was?"

"No, this one was a blonde girl. Very young."

"Ah. Cos Feargal's ok - quite decent, actually. He was very helpful to me when, when .. once," she finished lamely.

"I'll look out for the redhead then. And I won't talk to *anyone else*."

Mike nodded and put his hand over hers on the table.

"So I wonder what Roland was so afraid of?" Tamsin went on.

"We've been racking our brains about that morning, haven't we, Darling?"

"We certainly have. And there was definitely no sign of anyone when I looked outside. And if he went off again after bursting in, that suggests he hadn't actually *seen* anyone."

"Maybe he heard the swish of an arrow .."

".. and the thud as it embedded itself in a tree!" Verena couldn't resist, but shivered nevertheless.

"That would explain why there was no-one to be seen. Easy enough to remove the arrow again after frightening the bejasus out of him."

"Makes me squirm!" said Verena with a shudder.

"But who could it be?" Tamsin got up and shepherded the drowsy puppy into his crate along with the teddy bear he was falling asleep over, and returned to sit with her elbows on the table.

"Presumably someone who wanted the development stopped," said Mike firmly.

"Or someone who *didn't* want it stopped?" Tamsin raised an eyebrow.

"What do you mean?!" gasped Verena. "Wasn't he working for the developers?"

"It seems he was a bit of a maverick and was doing some investigating on the side."

"*Really?*" gasped Verena again. "So you're saying it could have been someone who was in favour of the plan, and wanted to stop Torben putting a spanner in the works?"

"Could be. It's hard to know who was on what side really. Perhaps we'll learn more tomorrow? Perhaps people will nail their colours to the mast at the meeting and we'll see who's who."

"Can't wait!" squeaked Verena. "I mean, it's awful - all this happening. All of it." She put on a suitably serious face. "But it needs to be resolved. We can't have murderers running loose, whatever their cause. Can we, Darling?"

Mike nodded again. "I hope that nothing untoward happens at this flaming meeting," he said moodily. "This is meant to be a quiet place!"

And with that, Tamsin dished out the week's homework sheets for them, said a few words of encouragement, all completely genuine, and fixed their next date.

Verena walked out to the van with her, and gave a cheery wave to a rider clop-clopping down the road from the top of the village. "There's Sara, out for her daily ride," she smiled. I actually go out with the barrow when she's been past, and collect fertiliser for the vegetable patch!" She waved vigorously and turned back to Tamsin, "Hard to recognise her in her riding gear and helmet - all those body and back protectors make her look twice the size! She's a slip of a thing without them," and as Sara approached, Tamsin waved too.

Sara stopped and said hello to both of them, before the phone rang inside the house and Verena saying, "Must go!" ran back inside.

"I wonder," said Tamsin, "could I ask you something, Sara? About your environmental campaigning?" The horse paced on the spot, chewing her bit, not happy her morning walk had been interrupted. So Sara slid off and led her to the verge where she could graze for a moment while she spoke.

"Yes? I'm keen on saving the planet before the previous generation of graspers destroys it. What would you like to know?"

"Well," began Tamsin slowly, "I know you and Roland were both active in that .."

"How do you know?" interrupted Sara.

"Let's just say I know. So you probably know that he was being chased on the Tuesday before he died - here in Bishop's Green. And I wondered, Sara, if he told you about what happened."

Sara chewed her lip and gazed across the broad village green - large enough to host a cricket match - its little pond and willows, and the majestic oaks, with the peaceful red rooves of houses peeping through their heavy branches, now bright with young green leaves. The original chocolate box scene.

"Since you know already. Yes. He said he thought someone was firing arrows at him. One narrowly missed him. He couldn't see who it was, but he ran for his life and burst into this house here to escape. Then," she poked at a clump of dandelions with the toe of her polished riding boot. "Then he thought he'd overreacted. He was embarrassed at barging into Mike and Verena's place, and he left again."

"And sadly they got him a couple of days later."

Sara wiped her eyes roughly with the back of her hand.

"I know you were friendly with him because of your shared interest, not as his girlfriend. Do you think you're in danger too? Or any of your fellow campaigners?"

"Anyone can take a potshot at me when I'm out on Crystal," she nodded to the horse who was now resigned to munching and had given up on her ride. "And no-one has. Yet. I make sure I wear all my protective gear when I'm riding. And as for the others, no-one knows who they are. We're very careful."

"I wouldn't be too sure about that," said Tamsin, thinking of the Coffee Shop Spy Network. "Thing is, this suggests that it may have been someone *in favour of* the development who killed Roland, and not one of the cottagers trying to defend their home."

"And who's the biggest supporter? My Dad. And Jackson. I really don't think they'll kill me, do you?"

"You can't think your father shot Roland, surely?"

"I wouldn't put it past him. He's greedy. I can't wait to get to Uni and away from all this."

"You'll miss Crystal?"

"I get your point. I was born with a silver spoon in my mouth. Yes. I'll miss Crystal. But perhaps one day I'll find a place of my own - something like those cottages with their acres. Or just a field for Crystal and a caravan for me. That would do."

"Until that happy moment? What are you planning?"

"We're looking at rural colleges - places where I can do environmental and animal stuff."

"That sounds fascinating - you'll enjoy working with the animals, I'll bet!"

As Sara remounted Crystal and started clopping forward again, Tamsin watched after her for a while, before turning back to her van.

But wait! What was that movement she caught out of the corner of her eye? Somebody behind the hedgerow? "I'm getting jittery!" she said to herself. "I'm imagining things ... or am I?"

CHAPTER THIRTEEN

She gave herself a mental shake and drove on to her next bit of investigation - the Misses Damson, at no.3. She was hoping that her appearance wouldn't alarm them and that word would have reached them about her recent presence in the village ... and she was not disappointed!

"Ooh, Marjorie! Look who's here!" exclaimed a chubby old lady in a sprigged frock who turned out to be the younger Miss Damson, as she opened the front door. "We were wondering when we'd get a visit!"

"We *were* wondering," echoed Marjorie, her older, thinner, sister.

"And now you're here - you simply *must* come in!" Miss Damson said, opening the door wide and causing two very fluffy cats to jump out of the way.

"I'll take our visitor into the parlour Edith, while you .."

".. put the kettle on. Right away!" Edith grinned childishly and walked slowly towards the back of the cottage, wading through cats, as Marjorie led the way into the parlour. "They must be well into their eighties," thought Tamsin as she ventured into the room which reminded her so much of The Furies' front room. More sisters living in a time warp.

The room was dark, with heavy lace curtains at the window. The paintwork was the same brown as The Furies' - the Misses Dodds as they were actually called. And the same clutter of ornaments and very old framed photographs filled every available space, except that taken up by sleeping cats.

"How many cats do you have?" asked Tamsin, twitching her nose slightly.

"Oh, about eight, I think ... " Marjorie waved vaguely at a chair, shooed a cat off it, which spat and strutted away, and offered Tamsin a seat.

"And have you lived here long?" Tamsin found herself embedded in the old and very deep armchair, and tried not to think how she'd ever get out of it again.

"For ever. We were born here. Our father was a ploughman, and he was very proud of being able to afford this little home for us."

"And it was just you two and your parents?"

"Oh no, dear. We had three older brothers. Two were lost in the war, in bombers, and the third - well, he went to Africa to find his fortune. It was a busy house." Marjorie's eyes gazed distantly at one of the photos on the mantelpiece. Tamsin made a feeble attempt to get up to look at it, made all the harder by the large spitting cat that had been displaced and was now filling her lap, and just peered at it from where she was.

"That's them?" she asked, seeing the photo of a group of cheerful young men beside a Lancaster bomber.

"That's them. Ronald and Graham." Marjorie said sadly. Clearly the loss had not diminished over the years.

"And the one in Africa?"

"Africa?" She frowned, then sat up straight and said quickly, "Oh yes! That was Simon. I mean, that *is* Simon. We haven't heard from him for such a long time." Marjorie gazed at her hands in her lap.

"Marjorie dear, could you help me?" came a distant cry from the kitchen.

"Here, let me!" Tamsin struggled to move the cat and get up, but was beaten to it by the spry Marjorie who, it must be said, had wisely opted for an upright chair.

After much clattering of tea things, the sisters appeared in the room again, this time with two trays which they placed on the only clear space on the lace-covered table by the front window.

"You pour," said one sister.

"I'll pour," said the other.

"You hand round the biscuits,"

"I'll hand round the biscuits."

And as she offered Tamsin a cup and saucer, Edith asked, "So we know just *who* you are, but what's your name?" and took a seat the other side of her.

"It's Tamsin, Tamsin Kernick. And thank you so much for inviting me to tea! I'd been hoping to meet you, ever since I discovered Bishop's Green and your delightful row of cottages."

"Delightful!" said Edith.

"Delightful cottages!" echoed Marjorie.

"We can see you love animals," Edith nodded at the large cat which had now been joined by another, almost burying Tamsin.

"And we can see you are fascinated by our little local difficulty," added Marjorie.

"Is it that obvious?" laughed Tamsin, stroking the second, friendlier, cat who was nuzzling her hand with its head.

"Why not?"

"Why not indeed?"

"Yes, you're right. I really feel for you - someone trying to throw you out of your home where you've lived forever."

"Forever," said Edith.

"Forever," echoed Marjorie, nodding vigorously, her long bird-like neck and her bird-like body so contrasted with her sister's more portly proportions, though they were both wearing identical summer dresses from an earlier age.

"And that was before the awful thing .. the murder," Tamsin ventured.

"Awful thing," they chorused.

Tamsin felt she was not just cemented in an armchair in a room from another epoch, but was also caught in an echo chamber. "So what do you think?" she ventured, deciding to cut to the chase with this pair of remarkable old ladies.

"It's all down to them folk up at the Manor," said Edith, pursing her thin old lips in her round face.

"Things never been the same since they came," said Marjorie, folding her hands in her lap with finality.

"You think they killed that poor man?" asked Tamsin, her mouth open to express her amazement, which she thought might be a good tactic.

"Bound to be them."

"Got to be them."

"It weren't any of us here."

"The Major said he told that man about the water creatures ..."

".. Who'd ever think beetles could save us!"

The pit-pat of comments continued, each sister completing the other's thoughts.

"He was friendly with that gel Sara from up at the Manor."

"And she's always putting up notices about saving the planet or summat."

"He must have been looking for them beetles .."

".. and got chased down to the river."

"That's what happened,"

"You mark our words."

"But we shouldn't say that," Marjorie terminated that line of thought.

"We'll get into trouble," giggled Edith.

Tamsin was beginning to feel she was watching a tennis match, as her head turned from side to side as she listened to each sister in turn.

"So you think it was the people who support the development - and the demolition of these cottages - who killed him?"

"Got to be," Marjorie repeated.

"But isn't everyone here an expert archer?"

"We don't join in firing them bows and arrows," laughed Edith girlishly.

"Doesn't everyone else?"

"No more does Pru!" said Marjorie.

"Couldn't say about Tom, though .."

"Yes, Tom might .."

"Anyways, there were lots of arrows wasted, so we hear,"

".. so it must have been someone who wasn't good at archery."

"Or someone pretending not to be?" asked Tamsin.

The two sisters sucked their teeth, looked at each other, and nodded.

"Someone pretending," they said in unison.

"Them folk up at the Manor are always shooting things .."

".. and shooting an arrow is the same as shooting a gun."

"They do say people get used to killing things."

"They do say it gets easier."

"Birds have a right to live, just like us."

"And cats," Edith nodded at the heap on Tamsin's lap.

Tamsin nodded slowly, beginning to feel dizzy as her head turned back and forth. "I see what you mean." What she could see was that the sisters were firmly pointing the finger at those who would disinherit them. Fair enough, she thought. But it doesn't really help.

"What will you do?" she asked her hostesses.

"We're going along tomorrow night,"

"Going to have our say,"

"We may be old but .."

".. we're not stupid!"

"We only hope that if they do go ahead .."

".. it'll be over our dead bodies."

"Oh, no more dead bodies, please!" exclaimed Tamsin.

"I remember a boundary dispute," Marjorie became more lucid, "when a man accused his neighbour of fencing off a tiny bit of his land."

"And they said, 'Is it big enough to bury a man in?'"

"'No? Then it's not worth bothering about.'"

"This is five acres .."

".. you could bury a lot of men here." Edith nodded, and Marjorie sucked her teeth again.

Tamsin looked at the Misses Damson. "I'm coming to this meeting tomorrow - I'll see you there." They may be old and poorly-educated, but they're canny alright.

She scrambled to her feet at last, shedding cats hither and yon - where had that small one come from? - made her goodbyes with many thankyou's, and set off on her way, not really any closer to a solution.

"What an odd collection of people in these cottages!" As she started the van she muttered to herself, as it was too warm to bring dogs with her today so they couldn't benefit from her wise thoughts.

CHAPTER FOURTEEN

Tamsin returned from her lunchtime dog walk with three worn-out dogs and a definite need for coffee. It was warming up to be a very pleasant "Flaming June", and she took off her cap and ruffled her hair.

"Perfect timing," she said as the dogs drank some water before stretching out on their beds with a big sigh, and Emerald drifted into the kitchen, pointing at the kettle, her head tilted questioningly.

"Up the Hills?"

"Yes. It was glorious today - beautifully warm with a stiff breeze. Clouds scudding about the place as they should. We went up Midsummer Hill. Thank you," she said, handing Emerald two mugs.

"Better get out another two - Feargal and Charity should be here in a moment."

"Already? I hadn't realised I was so long."

"Once you get up the Malvern Hills you step into another world."

"Just me? Or do you mean everyone?"

"Everyone, I think. It's a magical place."

"I'd planned on going up Pinnacle Hill, but Stockwatch showed there were loads of sheep turned out there this week. So we chose Midsummer

Hill, didn't we guys?" she got an answering thud-thud from Quiz's tail, followed by a theatrical sigh.

"Anyhow they'll be here soon so we can discuss strategy for tonight!"

"You're really into this aren't you? Where's your yogi avoidance of conflict?"

"I'm on the warpath for those cottagers. Sometimes we have to make a stand."

An eruption of barking meant that the dogs had heard a car pull up in Pippin Lane.

"You keep going with the coffee and we'll go and herd them in," said Tamsin and out she went, surrounded by a forest of waving tails, to greet their visitors.

Charity had brought Muffin, much to Moonbeam's delight, so the little dogs were dispatched to the garden for their game.

"I feel undressed," said Feargal, looking at all the livestock, after stealing a long look at Emerald making the coffee.

"Here," she said, "Have a cat!" and she passed Opal who had been lurking on the counter, "Don't feel left out." And cuddling the cat, Feargal followed the others into the living room.

"So what's the plan?" he asked, once they were all settled down with their drinks, and Moonbeam and Muffin had worn off their first excitement and come to find laps.

"I think we should operate separately," said Tamsin. "At least you should, Feargal. They'll know I know Charity, so we would naturally be together a bit. But I think we may learn more if we keep moving. Like, I bet you'd learn more from the Misses Damson than I did, Charity! I'm sure they've got more in their heads than they let on. Salt of the earth type, you know? Poorly educated but a solid set of values, I imagine."

"I'd love to chat to them! I'm sure we have a common history," Charity nodded vigorously.

"And Emerald could beguile all the menfolk," said Feargal.

"You make me sound like a lady of the night!" laughed Emerald in mock horror.

Feargal blushed fetchingly. "Oh no, not at all," he stammered in confusion. "I was thinking of those posh people up at the Manor, or maybe Jake of the veggie patch."

"I know," she beamed to soothe him. "I'm curious about this Jackson fellow. He seems a major player in the Manor set-up - I wonder where he stands in all this?"

"One thing I want to learn is Roland's domestic life," Tamsin put in. "If he had 'a woman in tow' as Lionel so snootily put it, where is she? Does she feature?"

"Good point," agreed Feargal. "And I'm going to do a lot of sniffing around the archery angle. Easy enough as they'll know I'm on the paper - though I'd better prevaricate over where I stand with the Cottage Campaign. I'll blame it on the Editor, suggest he's a bit of a lefty."

"Didn't I hear you're going to join the club, dear?" asked Charity, feeding a morsel of biscuit to Muffin on her lap.

"Well I'll ask if I can bowl along on Friday evening. Give it a try, sort of thing. I've done a bit before, you see, so I'm not a complete beginner."

"That means," said Emerald thoughtfully, running her finger round the top of her coffee mug, "that you'll be able to see who's good at it and who's not?"

"I should!"

"That's one of the things that keeps cropping up - in my mind at least." Tamsin chipped in. "Was the murderer really poor at archery, or just pretending?"

"All those arrows stuck in the ground?" asked Charity.

"Yes. Maybe they shot Roland first then fired a few about to make it look as though they kept missing."

"Do you have to be strong to fire an arrow?" asked Emerald.

"Not really," Feargal replied. "If you have the technique you don't need huge strength. And a decent bow helps."

"I thought the archers at Agincourt had to be super-fit?"

"Longbows are a big draw alright. And doing it repeatedly in the thick of a battle must be hard. And of course they had to march for days on hard rations to even get to a battlefield. But this person can't have been too far away from his victim. Wasn't Roland's body found fairly close to the road?"

Tamsin thought. "Not that far. Only about twenty-five yards. Not far at all."

"And presumably the killer was on the path, not at the entrance," added Charity, "so quite a close distance in fact. He'd have seen Roland's face .." she shuddered, as the enormity of the crime was brought home to them all again.

After a pause, Feargal said, "Targets for competition are usually at least fifty yards away. I believe the Olympics is about seventy-five."

"The things you know!" said Emerald.

"I have a reporter's memory. You wouldn't believe the jumble of strange facts and figures stored away in there!" he laughed.

"So it would be a big target for anyone at all good at archery?" asked Charity.

"I guess so."

"And a slow-moving target for anyone used to shooting game," added Emerald as she got up to offer a top-up for everyone, and went round with the cafetiere and cream jug.

"I think we need to look at motive. Off you get, Moonbeam," said Tamsin as she drew a notebook from her pocket, crossed her legs and made herself comfortable again. "There seem to be three possibilities that I listed." She read out her notes:

Anti development, pro Torben

Pro development, anti Torben

Anti Torben, uses development to cover crime

"Did I leave anything out?"

There was a general murmur of agreement, till Emerald said, "What about someone who got the wrong end of the stick? I mean, supposing one of the Antis thought Torben was in the pay of the Pros? They weren't to know about his secret mission with his environment buddies?"

"Great point!" said Tamsin, and rummaged down the side of the armchair cushion till she found a pen and added a line to the list. "Anti development, anti Torben," she said as she wrote.

"All that does is open up the field even more," sighed Charity. "It could be *anyone!*"

"Well I think the secret lies in the victim," said Emerald. I just feel sure it was a personal thing. I really don't think anyone wanting to stop the development would think killing a surveyor would help. They'd just send another. Unless it was a mistake. And one of the cottagers got it into their head that he was against them."

"Even then, they'd just send another surveyor, you're right."

"So it could be a personal vendetta," Feargal began.

"Or a crime of passion - in the moment," broke in Tamsin.

"It has to have been pre-meditated," said Charity slowly. "You don't wander round the place with a bow and arrows to hand in case you get annoyed with someone. It was planned - for whatever reason."

"And they could have been the bow and arrows stolen from the Major's shed for the purpose! Looks as though we're tending towards a personal motive. Someone using the development furore to get rid of someone," agreed Tamsin.

"Could be a rival of some sort?" ventured Feargal.

"Revenge?"

"Blackmail?"

"Heavy father?"

"We're going to have to do a lot of digging tonight!" Emerald jumped forward with enthusiasm.

"And I think it's our best chance," Feargal nodded. "Feelings will be running high, people's tongues will be loosened. I bet a lot of grievances will be aired."

"Right!" Tamsin stood up quickly, causing Quiz and Banjo to raise their heads and Moonbeam to jump about excitedly. "I have a couple of sessions to do today, and a report to write up. Let's reassemble, independently, at Bishop's Green Village Hall tonight!"

CHAPTER FIFTEEN

There was a huge hum of voices and bustle of excitement as people flowed into the hall - nearly full already by the time Tamsin and Emerald arrived. They'd seen Charity's car in the car park, but no sign yet of Feargal.

And when they entered the hall, the noise was deafening. The smell of many people was mingling with the traditional Village Hall smells of wood and polish. Most people were standing, talking loudly, gesticulating. Feelings were most definitely running high!

Tamsin and Emerald found a couple of seats without coats or bags on towards the back of the hall and staked their claim. "I'll just say hi to Verena over there - come and meet her."

Verena was in full spate, her eyes sparkling with excitement. "My dears!" she said, grasping first Tamsin's hand, then Emerald's. "Hello, hello Emerald! Enchanting name ... nothing as exciting as this has happened in Bishop's Green for years! Not since Lionel's tractor burst into flames on the top field and his man jumped out screaming blue murder. Can't *wait* to see what happens."

"Are you expecting something in particular to happen?" enquired Emerald.

"I've no idea! But it should be eventful." She turned and called to a neighbour and scurried off, pushing her way through the swell of people.

"There's Julia, with her two," Tamsin led the way over to where they were sitting. Julia looked nervous, Francine looked bored but scanned the room hopefully for boys, and Oliver was playing a game on his phone. "Hi Julia! How's Romeo?"

"Oh, he's doing marvellously at those things you've taught us in the house - I can actually get him to stop barking when the doorbell goes now!"

"That's great! Well done. Not so easy. Bet that's made a difference already."

"It sure has," interjected Francine, pulling a face.

"But he's still a nightmare when we're out ..." continued her mother.

"Don't worry, we'll start work on that tomorrow morning. We had to get the first things in place first - moving him from reacting mode to rational, listening mode. Softly, softly," Tamsin smiled, and as she turned she noticed Charity had already made herself at home with the Damson sisters who were both talking animatedly, antiphonally, as usual, one either side of her. She'll have a crick in her neck soon! Tamsin thought as she remembered the 'tennis match' she'd endured at the Damsons' cottage.

There was a knocking from the front of the room as the Vicar banged a book on the table in an attempt to call the meeting to order.

"I know this room is full of differing opinions and strong feelings," he intoned in a mournful voice, as the hubbub died down a little. "And I want to start out with a minute's silence for the terrible tragedy that occurred here last week. I will follow this with a prayer, to remind ourselves of our first duty as human beings." The congregation stilled. "I've chosen an ecumenical prayer that we all know," and after what seemed a very long minute while people stood with surprisingly little shuffling about, he straightened up and with a pause for dramatic effect, he declaimed "Our Father .." As he continued, most people joined in, bowing their heads and behaving themselves in readiness for the fray.

"Clever move," whispered Emerald.

His duty done, the Vicar went to a chair at the side of the hall, so as not to align himself with any party. And with much scraping of chairs, everyone who had a chair sat, the back and sides of the hall lined two- and three-deep with people standing. Amongst them Tamsin spotted Feargal, who saw her but showed no sign of recognition.

"Just how big is Bishop's Green?" Emerald asked her quietly, looking at the packed hall.

"Not this big!" whispered Tamsin. "These people must come from other villages round about."

"Perhaps it's Environmental-Rent-a-Crowd?"

Tamsin smiled and took the chance now to look over the heads of the people seated in front, and view the top end of the hall. There was a long table set out with four chairs. Behind it on the wall were four large pictures - those pictures developers think show an accurate depiction of their vision, all sunlit and light and green and leafy, with the corners of the red rooves of large houses barely noticeable amidst the mass of trees and shrubbery - which would presumably take years to grow. There was also a plan, showing a large entrance with automatic gates, winding drive-ways and spaced-out large houses, with those funny circles and blobs to indicate landscape planting. There was no sign of Jake's old fruit trees, or Pru's pond. And large fences round the gardens would prevent access to the stream.

"I'd protest on aesthetic grounds, never mind wiping out five histories in the process!" Emerald said to her quietly. "I wonder who's going to speak?"

Tamsin craned her neck so she could just see the name boards in front of each chair. "I think that large dark-haired man is the developer. Presumably the mousey-looking woman on the right is from the Council planning department. Oh! That's Lionel getting up - it looks as though he's going to chair the whole thing," and Lionel stood up, fastening his middle jacket button with one hand and smoothing back his greying hair with the other.

"Thank you Reverend." He bowed towards the Vicar. "Ladies and gentlemen - thank you for attending this public meeting. It has been called so everyone can see the plans for the new development, ask any questions they like of the developer, James Roscoe, and the council planning department - represented by Miss Eliza Timmins - and settle any misgivings you may have." He gestured to each of these worthies in turn as he spoke, the developer smiling expansively, and Miss Timmins rather more tersely, and both nodded in acknowledgement. "Some of us have lived here for many years, some are newer. But we all enjoy the peace and harmony of our village and wish it to flourish. I think we can all agree on that." He looked around meaningfully. "First of all, James Roscoe will outline the project. Mr Roscoe."

Lionel started clapping as he took his seat. The applause was taken up by only a few people in the hall, and petered out dismally.

"I think that shows the level of support for the plan," whispered Emerald.

After some murmurs and a little shuffling as people settled in their places, an expectant hush fell.

James Roscoe was a large man who looked sleek and self-satisfied. He explained how the project had come about through the death of the old landlord precipitating the sale of the freehold, he outlined the plans, and spent much time - using a pointer to pick out parts of the drawings behind him - emphasising the project's environmental impact, or rather the lack of it. He spoke of the need for villages to rejuvenate themselves, the importance of fresh people and ideas, the injection of cash into the local economy.

He was clearly attempting to lull everyone to sleep, but after ten minutes of this, some people were finding it hard to keep quiet and a man called out from the back, "What about affordable housing for the locals?" which brought a round of thunderous applause and stamping on the wooden boards, and some shouts of "Here, here!" and "Yeah! What about the locals?"

"I think this question is better addressed to the Council representative," he replied, and sat down smartly as he looked to the lady on his left.

Eliza Timmins had not been chosen for her ravishing good looks or her huge personality. She seemed as dull as ditchwater as she shuffled her papers and recited some platitudes about the plans for the county, their exemplary record to date of providing low-cost housing, issuing grants, and supporting local enterprise. She waffled on without giving eye contact to anyone in the room.

"But what about the people in the cottages?" shouted out a new voice from the side. "Who gives a damn about them?" called a voice from a few rows in front of Tamsin and Emerald.

"Incomers!"

"They'll turn it into a dormitory town!"

There were more shouts and as the meeting was getting increasingly raucous, a tall man stepped forward to the top table.

"I'm Rory Jackson. Many of you know me. I'm the Estate Manager at the Hall," he nodded towards Lionel. "And I'm also a Parish Councillor. And I can take a broader view. I can see how this development will benefit the community by bringing more wealth into the area .."

"More wealth into your pocket, more like!" called a large man in well-worn work clothes.

".. by contributing to the area and supporting us."

"Supporting the Manor, you mean!" a shrill voice piped up.

"Yes, the Manor's events will benefit of course, but you have to understand, I have the village's wellbeing close to my heart."

"You ain't got a heart!" a muffled cry came from the back.

Ignoring this, Jackson continued, "and more activity will bring more wealth. Many of you know about the Conference Centre we're building at the Hall. And these houses are necessary for the people who will work there."

"Jobs for the boys!"

"What about the workers?"

"And wasn't it handy for you that Roland Torben was *murdered?*" called out one brave soul.

Rory Jackson looked startled and peered into the crowd to see who had spoken.

"We all know he made off with your girlfriend!" shouted another.

"Got your own back, did ya?" jeered a third.

"You're handy with a bow and arrow, ain't you!" the shrill voice came in again.

"Everyone round 'ere's good at archery! You can't point the finger at Jackson," said someone in working clothes - possibly one of Jackson's men from the Manor Farm.

Major Cooper-Johnson jumped up, declaiming, "But safety is a most important part ..." but his attempt at defending his hobby was drowned out with jeering and he sat down again dejectedly.

Jackson's face turned angry as he squared his shoulders and faced the crowd at the back of the hall, "Are you suggesting ...?" he began, and got no further in the uproar that ensued.

The vicar stepped forward and spoke in Jackson's ear, then banged his book on the table again, calling "Order!"

But few people heard him over the commotion. Jackson pushed through the throng to the exit and left the hall.

Tamsin huddled close to Emerald as she spotted Sara at the back of the group of people along the side wall. She was with some young people who could be the environmentalists and tree-huggers, in their woolly hats and shabby anoraks. Sara was looking anxious - not surprising with the meeting breaking up in disorder all round her.

"The crowd's thinning out!" Emerald leaned towards Tamsin and grabbed her sleeve, turning her head to indicate the back wall.

"And getting slightly less noisy," agreed Tamsin, still looking at Sara, who slipped out of the hall with the crowd.

"I'm getting a bad feeling ..." Emerald said, holding Tamsin's sleeve tighter.

"Order!" cried the Vicar again, and this time his words got through. "We must remember our Christian duty to honour other people and allow them to air their opinions. Let this issue not divide our village!"

"It's already divided," Edith Damson's quavery voice spoke out into the hall. Heads turned in surprise as Marjorie echoed, "Already," and Tamsin could see little Charity just visible between the sisters, all three nodding vigorously.

Lionel stood again. "You've had an opportunity to see the plans, and hear what's being proposed. You can come up and inspect the diagrams closely now. You can make your opinions known by contacting the Council, who will take seriously all communications on the subject." He turned a questioning look towards the unprepossessing Miss Timmins, who gave a slight nod of assent. "All that remains is to say that I hope we will keep the Vicar's words in mind, and think of the future of Bishop's Green and the wellbeing of all who live here. Let me remind you, that as a magistrate, I don't want to see anyone up before me on Monday morning," he gave a nervous smile.

He shuffled his papers and tucked them into a folder, and turned to shake the hand of James Roscoe, whom he clearly knew fairly well, as they put their heads together and spoke out of the side of their mouths, clasping each other by the elbow as they took a long handshake..

Some of the audience rose to go up and study the pictures on the wall behind the tables, while others turned to exclaim to each other in varying degrees of shock and horror - much though some were enjoying the spectacle.

Tamsin saw Julia shepherding her two children - who both appeared dumbstruck - to the side door, avoiding the milling crowd at the back. There was no sign of Feargal. Presumably his news-hound's nose had led him out after Rory Jackson. And there was no sign of Sara either.

"How's your feeling?" she asked Emerald.

"Bad. I think we should go out. This is worse than I expected."

So they headed for the exit. Tamsin put a hand on Charity's shoulder as she passed, "You'd best stay put till the crowd has thinned out," and she smiled at the Misses Damson, still firmly seated beside her. "I'll see you outside when you're ready, Charity."

CHAPTER SIXTEEN

If Tamsin thought that things would be calmer outside the hall she was much mistaken! As her eyes adjusted to the gloom she saw that someone was lying still on the ground, a crowd of people hanging back in the shadows staring at the motionless shape, and Feargal was bending over the inert form of .. Rory Jackson!

"What happened?" she demanded, starting forward, Emerald close beside her.

"He's been knocked out," he said, straightening up and walking over to them. "And knocked about. There was a bunch of them attacking him when I came out. Too many for me to take on, so I pulled out my trusty football referee whistle, gave a blast on it, and shouted *'The police are on their way'!'"* He gave his cheeky smile.

"What?" he said to Emerald, who had folded her arms and was staring at him. "You wouldn't want me to mess up my face, would you?"

"So are they? The police? Are they coming?" pressed Tamsin.

"I called them," Verena said breathlessly as she joined them. "Disgraceful business. A lynch-mob!" she gasped. "Who knows where it could lead."

A dull groaning came from Rory Jackson, and Mike left Verena and went to inspect him. "Keep still, old chap. Help is on its way."

"Where are the people who did this?" asked Tamsin.

"Gone," said Verena.

"Vamoosed," said Feargal.

"Did you see who they were?"

"Nope," they both shook their heads. "It's dark this side of the hall."

"We've been asking for better lighting here for ages .." Verena protested, rather hopelessly.

The folk who'd remained in the shadows, gawping with curiosity, were now being joined by more people leaving the hall. And as the bee-baws announced the surprisingly quick arrival of the police, they were all corralled there and told not to move.

As the police started asking questions, Rory sat up, reached up to the back of his head, winced, and held his side instead. A first-aider stepped forward from the crowd and offered to take him to hospital. "Looks like you've fetched a broken rib or two, mate," he said.

Once the police had a preliminary statement from him, they despatched him with the first-aider, who was known to them from working at events in the region. He hobbled across the car park, supported by a person either side and was helped, painfully, into the car. Then the police turned their attention to the people they'd rounded up.

"They must think he murdered that bloke," said one, while another said, "Nah, reckon it's his own men saw their chance to duff him up - he's a mean so-and-so at work."

"It was those cottagers!" said another, pointing at the Major and Jake, the only cottagers present, Julia having slid out of the side door to get her children home, and the Misses Damson still safely ensconced in the hall with Charity.

After a few more pointed remarks and a few more questions, the police "invited" Jake to accompany them to the station.

"I ain't done it!" the gruff voice of Jake rang out. He lifted his brown hands up, "You can look at my hands - not a mark on 'em!" and Tamsin watched with her mouth open as they led the protesting market gardener to their Panda car.

"Surely he didn't do it?" she asked whoever may hear.

"I don't think he did," said Feargal, "but I couldn't say for sure."

"Who'll look after the chickens? And hasn't he a dog?" Emerald's thoughts went to what was, to her, the heart of the matter, as she pulled her coat tightly round her against the chill of the evening.

Major Cooper-Johnson said, "Don't worry my dear, I'll see to the animals. He'll probably be home very soon. Hope so, at least. Not like Jake at all. No reason for him to attack Jackson," he added thoughtfully.

"Then who did?" asked Feargal.

"Someone taking the chance to get their own back?" suggested Mike, who was back with them.

"He's not very popular," explained Verena, "a hard taskmaster, it seems."

"Does Jake work for him?"

"He's sometimes brought in for menial tasks. When they need a few more hands, you know." This from Mike. "Don't think Jackson rated him. Seems he caught him poaching on the estate once, and pays him very little to work in return for keeping his mouth shut and not reporting him."

Feargal shook his head slowly, "That's bound to build up resentment."

"Jackson's a big noise up at the Manor," added Verena. "Lionel depends on him. He's involved with all the enterprises up there."

"I can see why he's so vociferous in favour of this development. He sees money flowing into the estate coffers," Mike put in.

A thin voice broke in, "It's all so awful!" and they turned to see a very pale Sara standing beside them. "What's happening to this place?" and Verena stepped forward to comfort her as the tears started to roll down her face. "I'm glad I'll be leaving soon. They're all hateful," she started to sob.

As Verena led Sara away from the group, Tamsin turned to Mike, "So this Jackson fellow is not a fan of the cottagers?"

"Not one bit. Sees them as Luddites, parasites. I think he resents the fact that they've lived so cheaply for so long. Though in fairness, they get little from the landlord. They've made their own improvements to their properties."

Tamsin thought about what Jake had done in his acre, of Pru's pond and chickens, how Julia had painted the front of her cottage and grown a splendid garden, and the Major had built his shed and archery range. "It seems to me that there's a lot been festering here under the surface, and this building project has brought it all up."

"I'm afraid so," said Mike, watching his wife and the sobbing daughter of the Manor.

"And do you think it's connected?" Emerald asked the question in everyone's mind. "The murder and these plans?"

"It's hard to say. Someone had definitely put the frighteners on Roland. Remember his face that day at our house, Tamsin?"

"I sure do - haunting!" and she shivered. "It was as if he'd seen a ghost!"

The police started to shepherd everyone from the car park, and Tamsin watched them set off with their captive, his face white beneath his mahogany tan, staring out of the window with a desperate look in his eyes.

"Tamsin!" a familiar voice caused her to turn back to the hall, as Charity emerged. "Had a fascinating chat with those two old dears," she said. "They're barking, of course, but - as you say, salt of the earth."

"Glad you hit it off with them. Find anything interesting?"

"Just that they didn't hold with these newfangled building develop-ments, and it would happen over their dead bodies."

"Funny. They said that to me too. But I guess ... I mean, they're pretty old, aren't they."

"Prehistoric. And that comes from one who's not so far off herself," Charity smiled, her elfin features crinkling.

"You missed some drama out here!"

"I heard something had happened - police sirens and all that. Lionel made us wait in the hall till the coast was clear. "I got to talk to that lady from the council. And I mean 'talk to'. Could hardly get a word out of her. Don't know whether that's council policy or she just has no imagination."

"Well, the meeting was eventful alright!" said Emerald as they left the Major, who was delighted to find in Feargal another convert to the archery fold.

"But hasn't got us any nearer," added Feargal.

"See what you can find tomorrow night, Feargal. And I'm up here in the morning for a session with Julia, so I'm sure we'll learn more."

"Yeah, I spoke to the Major. Good fellow, if a bit of a caricature of himself. Very welcoming!"

"Hope that poor man gets home tonight .." Emerald looked from one face to the other. "He just doesn't look the type."

"Indeed," agreed Tamsin, "and I hope I'll be able to pick up some more strawberries and eggs tomorrow ..." And they made their several ways to their cars in the by now emptying car park, and betook themselves home to their beds. Truly the evening had been eventful.

CHAPTER SEVENTEEN

Tamsin slowed her van as she passed Jake's cottage the next morning, and was relieved to see not only a very full table of produce, but also Jake himself, bent over his courgette patch - lifting the large leaves to discover the secret courgettes below that were hiding to avoid capture and sneakily turn into marrows - and he was picking those that were ready. He looked up and she gave him a cheery wave. He stared back at her, grim-faced.

"He has no idea who I am," she confided to the dogs, "unless he saw me there last night. Glad he's back anyhow." And as she pulled in at No. 1, under the shade of a young birch tree, and turned off the engine, she heard Romeo bark several times before actually ... stopping! "Wahey!" she said to her flock, "it's working! Mind the car."

Quiz, Banjo, and Moonbeam recognised the words that meant she was leaving them for a while, and settled down to doze while she adjusted the window openings then made her way up the path with all its pretty, tangled, vegetation creeping across it.

Julia opened the front door with a beaming smile, as Romeo recognised Tamsin and bounded forward to meet her. "Look how he's keeping his feet on the floor now!" said Tamsin, as he sat before her, eyes shining, and she gave him a couple of dried sprats for his efforts.

"I have to tell you, he's been doing so well! You're such a clever little thing, aren't you Romeo?" said the doting Julia, as she led Tamsin into the kitchen. And she set about recounting all the marvels Romeo had performed since Tamsin's last visit. "You've certainly got a gift!"

"I just show you - you're the one doing the work. I'm delighted to see you're getting on better together."

"So do we start on the outside stuff today?" Julia turned to get her jacket and Romeo's lead.

"We'll start work on it, but right here in the kitchen first of all. How's he been on walks lately? Any improvements?"

"Ye-e-e-s," said Julia thoughtfully, "Yes, I feel less hauled about. He actually settles down and walks nicely after a bit."

"Great! We'll build on that. And once he's able to focus better it will build his confidence so he won't be so fearful. It's all connected!"

"Ri-i-ight," said Julia slowly, yet to be convinced. "But yesterday," she cast her eyes heavenward, "we passed the Damson sisters on the Green. They were trundling their cart thing about and gave Romeo quite a fright. Well, I mean, they do look strange, dressed just the same, same hair, they'd give anyone a fright ... Anyway, he didn't half bark at them! I had to drag him away. *So* embarrassing ..." she chattered on.

Tamsin set to work with her lesson, and when the hour was almost up was glad to accept the offer of coffee as Romeo slid gracefully onto his bed, his brain worn out from all he'd learnt.

"So! What do you think about last night's shenanigans?" she asked Julia, now busy making the coffee.

"Useless. We learned nothing new, really, and nothing constructive was said. It was ugly. Got pretty unpleasant when they were barracking Rory Jackson, that's why I thought it prudent to get the kids away before anything worse happened."

"So did you know that something worse *did* happen?"

"No! What?"

"They went from jeering and heckling Jackson to actually attacking him. They had to take him to hospital."

"*NO!*" Julia clattered the coffee mugs and cafetiere onto the table and sat down heavily in a chair. "Who? Who attacked him?"

"No-one knows. The police .."

"*Police?!*"

".. yes, the police came, and took lots of statements. But it seems the birds had flown."

"I bet it was his own men. There were a few of them there at the meeting. They don't like him, you know."

"Really? Hmm, you're not the first person to suggest that."

"Word has it that he's a bully. That's why his girlfriend left him - he was knocking her about."

"How awful! That's what someone said, wasn't it. And didn't they say she left him and chose Roland?"

"Apparently. I don't know. I know she'd had enough of Jackson. It may be true."

"You're right. The meeting didn't get anything further ahead, just underlined the chasm in the village between the yays and the nays,"

"The have's and the have-not's, I'd say," Julia pushed a mug across to Tamsin, who took the mug then shook her head, "It's a sorry state of affairs alright. What will you do if it does go ahead?"

"Have to try and find something affordable in Hereford, I guess. It's a mixed blessing. I love it here, but the kids are of an age when they want to be able to see their friends without Mummy having to fetch and carry them. It's the lack of public transport that's killing these villages, you know."

"That and the school closures."

"Not to mention the disappearing village shops and Post Offices ..."

"Speaking of which, you nearly lost your pop-up shop - they took Jake in for questioning over the attack."

"They didn't! How stupid. The man is softness itself. Talks to his vegetables all day, won't use any chemicals at all. Adores that hairy mutt of his. He won't eat his ducks either, they just die of old age eventually and he buries them. Won't even swat a fly."

"How does that fit with the poaching?"

"That's a point - never thought of it like that! Perhaps he reckons that's his birthright, as a countryman, and the rich guys shouldn't have all of it. Anyway," she said, "they got the wrong man."

"They must have realised that as he's home again now, I see. Good thing too, I have a shopping list!" As she stood up, she added, "Tell me, have you lodged an objection with the council?"

"We all did, when the idea was first put forward. The Major has been whipping us into action. That's why he was pleased when Torben appeared, and he was able to talk to him about beetles and water-courses and whatnot. But I don't think it'll do any good. I'll have to start a bit of house-hunting," she sighed, then they both laughed as the deeply-asleep Romeo started dreaming, uttering little stifled *wuffs* as his feet jerked about, chasing imaginary rabbits - or intruders with bows and arrows.

On her way to Jake's cottage, Tamsin noticed that the collection of beasts in Major Cooper-Johnson's front garden had moved about. Unnerving! Perhaps they got together at night for a chat and went back to the wrong places at sunrise? In the front window of the Damson cottage she could see two cats slumbering - one on the window sill and one on the ledge inside. Pru's cottage still seemed still and empty, though someone had made an effort to weed the drive. She wondered what the old lady made of all this brou-ha-ha happening while she was confined to bed.

Jake was not to be seen in his neat and productive front garden, though his table was laden. Had he seen her approaching and dodged out of sight? She went in and picked several items, leaving the money in the honesty box. The strawberries smelt gorgeous, and those courgettes he'd just picked couldn't be fresher, the cut stalks still moist! She sauntered back to the van, and greeting her happy dogs, said, "Hey guys! Fancy a walk?" the van walls clanged as the two bigger dogs' tails thumped them and Moonbeam started singing.

She drove well past the riverside walk - still too spooky, sadly - and found a bridlepath a mile or so further along on the Trumpet road. The weather had been dry recently, so it was firm underfoot. The dogs - dashing hither and yon - were absorbed in all the hedgerow smells as she made a mental note of the preponderance of brambles in flower which should yield a good crop of blackberries later in the year. Definitely worth re-visiting in September, she thought.

She looked up to see a hat bobbing along above the hedge, and called the dogs to her. As the bobbing hat got closer she saw it was a riding hat, on the head of ... Sara!

"Is Crystal ok with dogs? I can put them on lead if you like," she called out.

"No, she's fine thanks. She has to put up with Grouse at home, and yours are infinitely better behaved!"

"Have you recovered from that awful business last night?"

Sara clopped to a halt, sighed and her shoulders slumped. "I'm not sorry Jackson got what he deserved. He's always been a bully. But it wasn't nice. Not nice at all. I hate violence!"

"Yes, it was horrid. So do you think it was his men taking the opportunity to 'have a go'?"

"Probably. He doesn't have anything to do with the development as far as I know, except for getting £ signs in his eyes when he thinks of the estate business."

"And what about the shouts about him getting back at Torben?"

"It's true that Mandy left him and took up with Roland. And it's true that she told us that Jackson used to hit her. But why would Jackson want to kill him? It doesn't make sense. It certainly wouldn't bring Mandy back to him!"

"Strong emotions don't always make sense." Tamsin picked up Moonbeam so she could get a closer look at Crystal, who apparently smelt quite delicious.

"Is Mandy one of your environment friends?"

Sara sighed again. "How did you know, I still don't get it?"

"The coffee shop in Hereford, in the Old Market? Jeremy is a friend of a friend."

"Oh Lord. Well, there's no secret really, except from Dad. He thinks we're all tree-huggers and nuts."

Tamsin smiled. "Crystal's muzzle looks so soft and velvety ..."

"You're dying to touch it, aren't you! Go on, she'll enjoy it."

Smiling gooily, as only animal-lovers can, Tamsin stroked the horse's soft nose, cooing at her the while. "I don't think you're nuts. In fact .. I'd love to meet your friends. When are you next at Jeremy's cafe?"

Sara was totally seduced by the fact that Tamsin clearly truly loved animals. "You can come along tomorrow, if you like. Two-ish."

"Does Jeremy have a good selection of cakes?"

"Oh he does! The fudge and chocolate cake is my downfall!"

"Then it's a date! I might have a friend with me, is that ok?" She was thinking that Feargal would love to come along on this particular ride.

"Sure, as long as they are on the same page as us."

"Definitely. I don't think I have any property developers in my phone contacts," Tamsin grinned as Crystal snorted and tossed her head. "We must get on with our walks. Come on guys," she whistled up her troops. "Banjo, get behind," and she made room for Sara to ride on.

Entering the details in her calendar, she sent a quick text to Feargal before pocketing her phone again and focussing on the pure enjoyment of her dogs on this lovely walk. And she blessed the day she had first come to this area of central England, with its rural population, magnificent old buildings, and endless beautiful walks.

CHAPTER EIGHTEEN

"Great plan. c u there." Feargal had texted back, so the next day they met in the Old Market and made their way to Jeremy's cafe. They dawdled on purpose, admiring the delicious foods on offer in the trendy shops. They planned to arrive about ten minutes past the hour, to give Sara and her friends time to settle in.

"I've got loads to tell you about last night!" the real live Feargal now said, as they strolled through the busy precinct. "We can go over it all later. Oh look! An old-fashioned sweet shop!"

They gazed in the shop window like hungry orphans. "I have to get some of that marzipan before we leave!" Tamsin drooled like Quiz in front of a biscuit.

"I can't see this lot being involved in the attacks," said Feargal as they walked on again, Tamsin beaming over the prospect of chocolatey purchases. "I mean, I know campaigners can get carried away with their zeal, but I've been looking this crowd up, and there's no history of misdemeanours at all. Not even damaging railings by attaching themselves with bicycle chains, or blocking the public thoroughfare."

"Agreed. I can't imagine Sara doing anything bad. But I think there's more we can learn from them. I'd like to meet this Mandy, for a start," and Tamsin passed on the info she'd gleaned about the girl.

"Now that *is* interesting," said Feargal, "Can't stand men who knock women about," as they pushed the big door open, making a bell jangle, and entered Jeremy's lovely cafe. It had a different vibe from Jean-Philippe's, more rustic, with dried flowers and branches decorating the cornices, chairs with wicker seats, and soft browns for the wooden tables, in contrast with The Cake Stop's glossy dark ones. The walls were covered with huge images of the wonderful green landscape surrounding the city. It was warm and welcoming, and as they placed their orders, Tamsin gave a cheery wave to Sara who was already sitting with a group of anorak-clad friends.

"Let's share these!" said Tamsin, putting two plates of fudge and chocolate cake on the table with several forks. Faces lighted up at the invitation, and everyone shuffled up to make room for the newcomers.

Sara introduced them all, and on Feargal telling them he was involved with the Save the Cottages campaign in the paper, he was instantly accepted as a fellow spirit. They all tucked in to the cake, and after a while, Tamsin said, "So what do you think of this business on Thursday night?"

"If you ask me," Mandy said eagerly, "Jackson got his come-uppance!"

"Yeah, bullies should get a taste of their own medicine," said the smallest anorak, who perhaps had personal experience.

"Were you all there?" asked Feargal.

"Yes," they all murmured. "We wanted to object to the development .."

"And to see if we could find out who'd killed Roland!" said Mandy. "It wouldn't surprise me if it was Jackson, getting his own back."

"For what?" asked Tamsin.

"I used to be with Rory. But I couldn't stand his arrogance after a while."

"Or the bruises," added Sara, putting a hand on Mandy's arm.

"Or the bruises," she agreed, folding her arms close round her body and rubbing the remembered bruises.

"Is he the jealous sort?" asked Feargal.

"Thinks he's God's gift." Mandy replied through thin lips.

"But would he kill someone? I mean, what good would it do? It would hardly bring you back."

"No, I suppose not. If he'd just whacked him I could believe it. Anything small or fluffy or feathered is fair game to him, and he's certainly a harsh taskmaster up at the estate. But you're right. He's not a murderer."

"It wouldn't surprise me if you wanted to get back at him, there in the darkness ..." Tamsin floated the idea.

"I was angry with him, yes. But I'd only started going out with Roland fairly recently. It wasn't that big a thing. It's awful that he died, but I'm not wearing widow's weeds. Oh, that sounds so callous .."

"We know what you mean," Sara soothed her. "Roland wasn't the love of your life."

"No. But he was a good bloke, and so gentle. Such a welcome contrast to Jackson. He helped me get a job here in town, and a place to live. They'd better find out who did it and throw the book at them!"

"We don't hold with violence," said one of the scruffier guys, with a knee-jerk response to book-throwing.

"It's part of our mission - to harm nothing and no-one," said another.

"Roland wanted to preserve the special environment of the cottages,"

"And save the water-beetles! Did you know they're an endangered species?" demanded the fourth campaigner.

"I know little about insects," said Tamsin apologetically. "But I do realise the importance of saving them and their habitat."

"It's all so horrible," Mandy looked close to tears. "I thought I'd escaped a bad situation and found some real friends - I mean I *have* found real friends - only one has been taken away from me."

Sara put her arm round Mandy's shoulders, and the young men looked uncomfortable and fiddled with the spoons and sugar packets.

Feargal held out his card to Sara. "If you can think of anything -

anything at all - that can throw light on this, do let me know. It all fits in with the Cottages campaign. The *Malvern Mercury* wants to see justice done!"

After this little speech, he and Tamsin rose and made their goodbyes.

Tamsin found herself making directly for the marzipan shop, and busied herself with her choices before they headed for the van where she unwrapped her first purchase and eyed it gluttonously, while Feargal started telling her about the Archery Club.

"It's a quaint group, alright!" he began, smiling at the memory. "I enjoyed it a lot - forgotten how much fun it is. And it's like riding a bike, you don't forget how to do it once you've learnt. I was surprised how quickly I was hitting the target again, after years without touching a bow, really surprised! The Major runs it, and he's right - he's an absolute stickler for safety. Forever counting heads to be sure no-one's drifted behind the targets, into the firing line. There were a couple of young boys there - super keen. And safety is baked in to his teaching."

"He wasn't putting it on for you?" Tamsin nibbled a little of the chocolate-covered marzipan and offered Feargal some.

"No thanks," He shook his head, "I don't think so. The way he was teaching the boys, and the way they demonstrated that they knew the safety protocol was pretty convincing. They just did it all automatically."

"What kind of protocol?"

"It's very disciplined. Everyone has to be behind the shooting line, not at the sides in case an arrow deflects off the target. I saw a couple of arrows do that. No-one may shoot till given the instruction by the captain. They can only shoot from the shooting line - they can't even nock an arrow until they're on that line .."

"Knock an arrow?" Tamsin licked her fingers.

"Nock - no K at the start. It means hitching it up into the firing position."

"Ah, gotcha."

"And the Field Captain - or Field Major in our case!" he laughed, "gives the order when they can go and collect all the arrows. The safety issue really is a strong point. No-one who goes to that club would be in any doubt how dangerous these arrows are."

"Hmm. So who else was there?"

"Julia and her two. Jake. A couple of workers from the estate ... let me think - yes, the father of one of the young boys. Um .. The bored sister of one of the boys .."

"Hardly murderer material."

"Oh, and apparently Jackson often comes. But of course with a broken rib he wouldn't be able to do much. He wasn't there last night anyway."

"Were any of them any good? Any bull's-eyes?"

"Jake's pretty handy. I think he probably uses his bow and arrow for poaching. Apparently he's won a few prizes for field archery - you know, when they shoot the model animals."

"The ones in the Major's front garden - yeah, creepy!"

"Jake would be a silent assassin - not scare the animals off. And it's kinder than using traps - those are pretty ghastly."

"True. And illegal. Who else was good?"

"Julia's son Oliver is really good. Got a great eye. But I think we can safely discount him! He's only nine, after all. He's school-friends with the other two boys there."

"What about the men from the estate?"

"One was pretty handy, the other's a beginner. But they hate Jackson, and Jackson is in favour of the development, which none of the born-and-bred locals seem to be."

"Probably a case of 'any enemy of Jackson is a friend of mine'," Tamsin stowed the rest of the marzipan in her bag.

"Agreed. I think that rules them out for Roland. But the bigger of the two men had bruises on his knuckles. He kept his hands in his pockets most of the time, but I saw them when he was shooting."

"So that makes Jackson's attack look fairly well accounted for. A very strong surge of ill-feeling though!"

"I think it was exacerbated by the passion of the meeting."

"And the fact that the men had been in *The Goat and Compasses* since opening time ..."

"Maybe beating up Jackson was a kind of displacement activity seeing as they could get no sense out of the meeting itself."

"Did you hear any more about the stolen bow and arrows?"

"Not directly. The Major made a big show of unlocking the shed and padlocking it again when they finished, with his shiny new padlock. I don't suppose he ever thought he needed to lock up the shed before. The recurve bows are all taken down at the end of practice, so only someone who knows how to put them together again would have any use for them: it's actually very hard to attach the string. The boys all had to be helped by an adult. And he trusts his club members."

"I don't suppose any of them lock their doors," mused Tamsin. "Back in Brum it was like leaving Fort Knox when we left the house. I'm much more casual here - though I do turn the key in the lock when I go out. There are often valuable dogs there," she smiled.

"Though nothing much else worth stealing," Feargal winked.

"So where are we now?" asked Tamsin with a mock-angry face, starting the engine and pulling away from their parking spot.

"Nowhere." Said Feargal glumly. "All roads lead to nowhere."

"I don't buy the Jackson-Torben angle. He just doesn't look caring enough to harp on about Mandy leaving."

"No more do I. And I'm more than ever convinced the answer lies amongst those cottages. This development ... oh, I don't know."

"We've cut a lot of people *off* the suspect list. But there aren't really very many *on* it. And those that are - we-e-ell, the possible motives are pretty thin."

"We've experienced and learnt so much in the last couple of days," Feargal stretched his long legs as far as he could in Tamsin's small van. "I think we should focus on having a relaxing Sunday tomorrow and let it all filter through the back of our minds. I think something will appear soon enough."

"Got to. Charity's putting a brave face on it. But I know she desperately wants to know who killed Roland Torben, so that it's proven that it's not her."

"I noticed her hobnobbing with some of the older folk on Thursday night."

"Yes, she seems to have befriended the very strange Damson sisters. If there's anything to be learned there amongst the cottagers, I'm sure she'll tell us soon enough."

And they drove the empty back roads and admired the hedgerows, now sporting a beautiful show of cow parsley, dog roses weaving through the hawthorn, and morning glory winding around everything - its trumpet flowers splendid in the late afternoon sun - back to Malvern.

CHAPTER NINETEEN

Monday found Tamsin negotiating the sheep obstacle course up the long drive to Bishop's Green Manor House. It was time for Grouse's second lesson, and she was bursting with curiosity about how the latest events had gone down in the big house.

It was clear from the moment the door opened and Grouse came bounding out and jumped all over her van, his claws gouging her paintwork - ignoring the barked commands from his cross owner - that no homework had been done. She sighed and realised she would have to adopt a firmer position. There was no point them paying her to come and do things with their dog if they wouldn't do things themselves. "People are always wanting a magic wand," she sighed to Banjo, who was accompanying her today. A tail swish indicated his sad agreement.

Once they'd arrived in Lionel's office - made difficult with Grouse trying to trip them over, and Lionel still fruitlessly shouting at him - Tamsin set about the lesson. She was much more sergeant-majorish in her teaching Lionel, and emphasised the relation between the exercises she was teaching and Grouse's general attitude and behaviour.

"We don't want to squash his enthusiasm!" she assured Lionel. "But we do want him to listen."

"I think Labradors' ears share a neural connection with their legs. Once one is working, the other is not." Lionel said huffily.

"Let's get some new neural pathways formed!" Tamsin laughed, and continued to coach him. And they actually made some headway. Finding Lionel receptive to this new attitude of hers, she worked out a timetable for him. Clearly Felicity had not held him to the last one she had loosely suggested, so this time she went through each day with him and located a spot where he agreed to do some training, writing down the time of day beside the exercises.

"Mostly you can do this in 30-second bursts at any time. Every time you see Grouse you can ask him to do something - even just look at you, and reward him. He'll soon start paying you more attention, won't you Grouse?" she added as she ruffled the big head that was right beside her knee. He clearly found this nicer, friendlier, cheese-scented, person worth cultivating.

"I don't hold with all this giving treats all the time," Lionel objected.

"Well, as I said, you have to feed him anyway, so make the food work for you," she smiled sweetly in response. "And tell me," she said as she started packing away her things, "how is Mr.Jackson?"

This opened the floodgates. "Disgraceful business. Absolutely disgraceful. He has a broken rib - and concussion. So now I'm a man down right in our busy season."

"Is he pressing charges?"

"He can't identify with certainty who it was, though he says he has a fair idea."

"Is it true what they're saying? That it was a disgruntled worker?" she asked tentatively.

"Maybe," said Lionel uncomfortably. "Perhaps he'll temper his dealings with his men now. Some of them have worked here for ages - got tied cottages - don't want them all getting upset. I can't see it being them anyway. Much more likely those scruffy anoraks Sara hangs out with."

"Why would they want to attack him?"

"Anti-progress, that's what they are. And Jackson is overseeing all the improvements we're making. Dashed lefties ..."

"I suppose feelings were running high because of the meeting, and just .. overflowed?"

"Still disgraceful. We have weddings booked. Poor Felicity's having to do loads more work."

"That's the way, I suppose, with a family business? But surely Felicity is very capable, that's how she struck me!"

"She is, yes. Great gal."

"And Sara? Does she chip in?"

"Not really. Too young and self-absorbed. Not interested. Sooner she gets to University and starts working the better. She can work all this student protest nonsense out of her system and settle down to something productive."

Tamsin wondered what exactly Lionel had in mind for his daughter, though it probably included marriage and horse shows. Don't think that's going to work, she thought to herself.

This time there was no invitation to the kitchen, but as she went out to her van she bumped into Felicity coming round the corner of the building wearing gardening gloves and carrying a large sheaf of flowers. Despite working in the garden, she still looked the epitome of the well-heeled country lady. She greeted her warmly, "I hear you're up to your eyes in Mr.Jackson's absence?"

"Oh I am, yes." Felicity stopped and shifted her load of flowers from one arm to the other, passing a hand over her damp brow and tossing her hair back. "What a palaver!"

"Not much good came from that meeting, did it?"

"It just served to stir things up further. Why people want to stand in the way of progress I can't imagine."

"I guess the development is key to your conference centre going ahead?"

"No, we'll still do that - but it would help a lot to have those sort of people actually living here. We'll need educated staff."

Tamsin let this stinging condemnation of their present workforce go, and instead asked in a confidential voice, "Who do you think attacked Mr.Jackson?"

"Got to be that rabble who came - rent-a-crowd troublemakers if you ask me. I hope the police will be dealing with them."

As Tamsin made her goodbyes and slid into her van, she said to Banjo, "Let's get out of here kiddo. The intolerance and entitlement levels are too much for me." And they trundled through the sheep again, avoiding a gang of gambolling lambs who seemed to be playing chicken at the side of the road - waiting till the last moment before dashing out in front of her van - and went to the orchard near Bingham Parva for some peace and quiet at one of her favourite haunts.

And she was pleased to see Maggie's car already parked there. She and Banjo set off on their walk and it wasn't long before she saw Maggie and Jez walking towards them. As Banjo needed time to get used to strange dogs, she left him in a down as she advanced to say hello to Jez.

"Missed you at that little local excitement last week," said Tamsin as they walked on together, Banjo content to keep his distance.

"It was packed! I saw you sitting with your blonde friend, the one we met on your big dog walk,"

"Emerald."

"Emerald, that's it. No," she wrinkled her freckled nose, "it was not at all productive - pretty much a whitewash really, and Don got a call while the woman from the council was talking but not saying anything, so we left early."

"Ooh, you missed the main attraction!"

"I heard about it. Had to go in to the police station with some papers, and they were talking about it there. Then of course your friend wrote it all up for the *Mercury*," she smiled.

"That's what he does, I guess! On the spot reports - good for his advancement, I believe, having a nose for being in the right place."

"It seems there's some deep ill-feeling in that village. Not good. Not good at all."

"There's a lot more than meets the eye - but that goes for any village, I suppose. It's one of the advantages of living in a small town as I do, that these grievances don't seem to seethe below the surface. There's more movement in the population, I guess, so historic resentments die out. I found out all the historic resentments the hard way, over in Nether Trotley not so long ago."

"Indeed! So are you any nearer knowing who fired the fatal arrow, Tamsin?"

"At the moment I learn something new every day! But none of it makes too much sense. People are quick to point the finger, but there doesn't seem to be much in the way of supporting evidence. No proof."

"What's your latest intelligence, then?"

Tamsin paused to observe Jez and Banjo both sniffing in the same area. Banjo quietly moved on and left Jez to it, and she said "Good boy, Banjo," before turning back to Maggie. "It seems the fellow that got hit on the head is a bully. His men don't like him, and his girlfriend left him - she was getting knocked about."

"Good for her! So?"

"She left him to take up with Roland Torben. The fella on your slab."

"In a drawer now, actually, but carry on. That's very interesting."

"And she's also tied up with the environment objectors. It's all wheels within wheels."

"So maybe her new friends - who were there in force on Thursday I saw - had a go at Jackson?"

"I'm not sure - they seem to be peaceable tree-huggers. But maybe his estate workers - who were also there in force - took advantage of the general tone of the evening to give him a taste of his own medicine? He's a bully and a tyrant to work for, apparently."

"Either way it doesn't get us any nearer the phantom archer!"

Tamsin sighed, and called Banjo in as they reached their cars again. "That's still a mystery. But I hereby declare," she laughed, raising her right hand, "that it will not remain a mystery for long!"

"Just take care, Tamsin. Somebody is either mad or dangerous, or both. Keep out of their way!"

"I'll do my best. I don't wish to become a statistic - or visit your post-mortem room in a professional capacity!"

"Seriously," Maggie waited while Jez hopped into the car, then shut the boot and came to look Tamsin in the eye. "Whoever did that to that young man will not hesitate to kill again. I've seen too much in my line of work."

Tamsin took the offered hand, squeezed it and said, "Understood." And jumping into her van she leaned her cheek against Banjo's soft muzzle before driving on.

CHAPTER TWENTY

Tamsin spent the morning doing paperwork and accounts - with much sighing and exasperation - and was relieved when Emerald did her floaty thing down the stairs, accompanied by the soft pad-pad-pad of Opal, giving her an excuse to stop and make coffee.

"I could hear that sighing all through my yoga practice," said Emerald, as she greeted all three dogs, who'd been lying low while Tamsin worked and cursed.

"I don't think I'll ever get on with numbers and spreadsheets and whatnot," Tamsin shrugged. "I do try to keep ahead of it all. Terrified of losing track then getting a whopping tax bill."

"Like me! I didn't start my yoga classes in order to run a business! I just wanted an excuse to do yoga all day - and help people to a better life."

"You and me both. Ah well," Tamsin poured the coffee and handed her friend a mug, "'tis the price of success!" and they adjourned to the garden.

"So what's the latest?" asked Emerald, sitting on the grass as usual, Opal settling in her lap, while Tamsin chose the bench. "You went to the scene of the crime again yesterday, didn't you?"

Tamsin paused while she balanced a treat on Banjo's nose. He went delightfully cross-eyed as he froze in place waiting for his release. "Gettit!" she said, and he tossed the treat in the air and snapped it cleanly.

"They're so quick at that," Emerald admired.

"Yes, they love doing things that test them. And yes, I went to the Green again. Saw Maggie too, on a walk. She's worried I'm going to end up D.E.D as well. Bit unnerving ..."

"I know you. You won't let go till you've solved this mystery. Not for nothing are you Tamsin the Malvern Hills Detective!" She lay back on the ground and stretched her long legs up in the air.

Tamsin laughed and accepted Opal onto her lap, who was clearly needing to try a more secure spot. As the cat purred she felt soothed. "I've got my Nether Trotley class tonight. Amazing how well that's going after a pretty shaky start."

"Shaky? That's one way to describe it!"

"In that case there were no apparent culprits. Couldn't find it out - for what seemed a long time. But in this case there are plenty. It's a question of eliminating those who couldn't or wouldn't ..."

"And nailing those who could and did."

"No nearer yet. But .. I'm turning it all round in my head. Something is going to click at some stage, hopefully before Maggie has to start doing her patchwork on me."

"Don't." In one graceful movement, Emerald sat up again, tucked her long and shapely legs under her, picked up her mug and sipped her coffee. "You've come to know everyone there by now, haven't you?"

"More or less. I've barely met the Major, but Feargal spent an evening with him at the Archery Club session on Friday. He doesn't think it's him. In fact, he didn't find any likely perpetrators at the practice."

"You have to get the lingo right if you're going to play this game," Emerald smiled, "It's 'perps'."

"Sadly it ain't a game. Perps. Isn't that American? Shows what you watch on telly."

Ignoring the remark, Emerald asked, "What does Feargal think? He's pretty sharp usually."

"About as little as I think. Not a lot. Except he thinks it's all to be found in the cottages somewhere. I'm convinced of that too. I think everything else is a bit of a red herring."

"And you've worked through the suspect sheet, all the cottagers, right?"

"Well Pru is not yet back from the hospital or nursing home or wherever she is, but I gather her son's been around. Very pro the development. Clearly doesn't care much for his mother's beloved garden and pond and chickens and all. She'll struggle to find something else as good as what she has, I guess." She started stroking Opal pensively, causing her motor to start up again into raucous purring. Quiz came over and inquisitively poked the cat's side with her muzzle, which Opal totally ignored and purred ever longer and louder. "Then the others - I can't see Jake doing anything violent. Surely Julia and her kids are out of the frame. Feargal says the Major's a good egg - and fanatical about safety and protecting the good reputation of his sport. Then the old ladies - they're dippy if you ask me. But harmless."

"Hmm. Somebody's hiding something. And hiding it well."

Tamsin poured Opal onto the floor and got up. "I'm taking this lot out for a walk. Thanks for the break. I'll carry on doing sums another day. I've had enough for one morning!"

And she enjoyed a wonderfully peaceful walk on the Common, the majestic Malvern Hills towering above her so close by - like ancient guardians protecting her - and watching the hang-gliders floating about high above. As she started back, she spotted a familiar pair coming down the hill. "Charity! Muffin! Hello there!"

Muffin raced towards her, giving her a peremptory greeting while intent on finding her chum Moonbeam. Charity joined them and smiled broadly as the two small dogs hurtled after each other in big circles, watched by a bemused Quiz and disinterested Banjo. "I wondered if I'd find you here, dear," she said, "I'm a bit stuck on Muffy's new trick. Can you help me out?"

"Of course! Love to. It's the pulling off your clothes one, isn't it?"

"Yes. She's doing so well at the pulling part. I taught that separately with an old cloth, as you told me to. It's just getting her to understand when she can grab my sleeve to pull."

"Gottit. Ok, let's see what you've got so far." And Tamsin revelled in doing what she did best - finding the tiny missing link that made all the difference to the smooth working of the trick.

"So," she summed up after their short training session, "Muffin knows she can't normally grab your sleeve. So it's just a case of transferring the cue of 'Pull' from the cloth to what you're wearing. Your word 'Pull' will mean 'pull the nearest bit of cloth', as you hold out your arm. She doesn't want to do the wrong thing, that's why she's hesitant. You're a good girl so you are, Muffin!"

"Thank you so much! I wasn't terribly wrong then?" Charity asked anxiously.

"Nope. You were terribly right. And Muffin was even righter," laughed Tamsin. "You just needed an adjustment, that's all. You're doing great - and I think it'll be a really handy thing for you, specially if you ever get a sore back. It was so useful for me when I got a bad bout of tennis elbow once and struggled to get out of a coat. That reminds me, I should brush up that skill with them - Quiz and Banjo are good at it, but Moonbeam hardly knows it. Once I've taught something to one dog I kinda expect the others to learn it by osmosis! There, that's my homework for the week!"

As they walked together towards the road, Charity asked after Jackson. "Any news? Such an appalling thing to happen!"

"He's still off work apparently, and was too incapacitated to attend his usual archery practice," Tamsin raised one eyebrow meaningfully.

"Really? Another possible then. Though why he'd do in that poor young man - unless he was acting on instruction from his boss ..."

"I never thought of that! Now you've put up a hare, Charity."

"Fathers can be so possessive. And it seems to me that Lionel is quite the controlling type of person. It never works you know. The girl always manages to escape - if she has any gumption at all."

"Sara has plenty of gumption! All she wants is to get away, and take her horse with her."

"Not much chance of that at University, I wouldn't have thought."

"I think that's her distant dream. But she's a determined person. She might just work it out. I was at her place yesterday, but I didn't see her."

"I'm going that way myself on Thursday! I've been invited to tea by the Misses Damson. Marjorie and Edith. They're so quaint."

"I wish you good luck with that," Tamsin said fervently. "You'll feel as if you're sliding inexorably back through time. Very strange sensation, I found."

"They said they'd love to meet Muffin too, so I'll be able to take her," she cast a loving look at her fluffy little dog trotting along beside Moonbeam.

"Muffin's good with cats of course, being used to your collection."

"Oh yes, I assured them of that. I hope their cats don't mind."

"They should be used to dogs, with a dog each end of the row of cottages. Let me know how you get on! You might just pick up a bit of info that takes us further."

"Of course. And see you this evening, at Trotley."

"See you there," smiled Tamsin happily as she gathered her clan and headed towards the road and home.

CHAPTER TWENTY-ONE

"Feargal's here already," said Kylie after she'd taken Tamsin's order. She nodded her head towards the darker end of The Cake Stop. Tamsin inhaled the rich scent of the cafe, the sweetness of the cakes mingling with toasted cheese and ciabatta, all overlaid with coffee of every kind. And she smiled at the quiet mood music, the subdued chatter of the patrons and the occasional clatter of spoon on plate..

"He always likes to lurk," laughed Tamsin, "while I like to sit in the comfy armchairs at the front and watch the world go by." She looked longingly at the cake shelves. "What's that one at the front, with pale green icing on the top?"

"The Furies' latest concoction - Pistachio. Looks gorgeous, doesn't it."

"Oh my, I have to have it! Give me two forks so at least Feargal will wolf down most of it."

"And I'm sure Moonbeam will enjoy licking your fingers for you," Kylie grinned as she dished up a mammoth slice of cake and leaned over the counter to smile at the little dog.

Feargal gave her an equally large grin as she arrived at his table. "Wotcher!" he said, as he pushed the chair opposite him out from the table with his foot, and "Hey, that looks good," as he reached to grab a fork. There followed a few moments of munching while they savoured the cake, before Feargal put his fork down on the empty plate with a flourish and stretched back in his chair, watching with amusement as Tamsin squashed a crumb onto the tip of Moonbeam's nose and the little dog licked it enthusiastically.

"What news from the battlefront?"

"I was over at Lionel's on Monday," Tamsin began, then related what she'd learned there. "So we have more insights into the Manor House setup - that Jackson's a bully, Lionel's going to curb his excesses to keep his men sweet, and that Sara wants to leave asap. I get the feeling that Felicity's trying to stay on the fence between Sara and her father, preserve the family feeling, you know?"

"Nothing much new there," said Feargal, squashing the remains of the icing on the plate with his fork, and making designs in it.

"Oh, and I ran into Maggie too - you know, the pathologist."

"Ah yes, and what did she have to say?"

"Worried that I'll end up next to Roland in her Post Mortem Room. Made me shiver, I have to say."

"Can you make sure you've always got a dog with you?"

"I can on walks - not that that's much defence against an arrow, but when I go to people's houses I can't. Which reminds me, I'm back at Bingo's tomorrow."

"Who?"

"Bingo. Mike and Verena's puppy. Where it all started, for me."

"Ah yes. Verena. She was up to 90 at the meeting. Loving it!"

"She was! But I think that she's shocked at what's going on now. Just loves a gossip, that's all. Not after any serious aggro."

"It *is* shocking, such violence in such a pretty place," he mused. "We've had all sorts of nuts coming out of the woodwork since we started the cottage campaign on the paper."

"Don't you always?"

"Yep. Goes with the territory. But two of them said the same rather odd thing, which was surprising." He leaned forward, his elbows on the table. "Seems that some people think that's not the first violent death in the area."

"Say more!"

"They didn't say any more. Just a kind of 'you mark my words' sort of thing. Anonymous, so I can't follow up."

"Anonymous? That's clever of them, these days."

"Notes that came in the post. You can still stay anonymous that way."

"So I guess you've hunted through the records?"

"I have - to no result, and my contact at the police station can't find anything either."

"Aha! Your mole. I'd love to know who it is," grinned Tamsin.

"You'll have to remain in blissful ignorance," said Feargal with a smug expression. "A journalist never .."

".. reveals his sources, I know!"

"*If* it's true, it suggests that someone disappeared at some stage, and some people wondered .."

"That *is* interesting. Perhaps we should do some sniffing as to who may have vanished suddenly?"

"Could be from years back. The style of the handwriting on the notes suggested that the writers were quite old. Could be an unwanted baby, rather than an adult. That did happen quite a lot back in the day."

"I suppose it could. There are advantages to our modern welfare systems, even though some people resent their snooping."

"If it was a long time ago, that would rule out Julia, and the Major. They haven't been there that long."

"True. But the other cottagers have been there for ever."

"Oh look, isn't that Charity over there? She's working the room like a politician!"

"Charity knows everyone!" laughed Tamsin, and catching her eye she called her over - which didn't take long once Muffin had caught sight of Moonbeam and heaved her owner along behind her - weaving through the chairs - for a joyous reunion.

"Charity, *you* love sniffing about," began Feargal. "We've had some anonymous notes. It seems that some people are suggesting there's been a previous death in Bishop's Green, perhaps a long time ago, and it was never picked up or investigated."

"Fascinating! Well I'll certainly see what I can discover. I'm visiting two of the oldest residents tomorrow. If anyone knows, they probably do."

"The sisters," Tamsin explained for Feargal's benefit. "I wonder if they wrote the notes?"

"Perhaps I'll get them to write me out a recipe or an address or something. Then you can compare the writing!"

"Charity! You've been watching too much tv!"

Charity gave a wicked smile, "And I may take a stroll round the village, see if I run into anyone else while I'm there."

"Do take care, Charity! Maggie - you know, one of those doctors from Bingham Parva - she's convinced there's going to be another murder."

"Watch out for mad archers!" warned Feargal cheerily.

"Well, I think we should take Maggie's words seriously. She's worked with the police for ages. Must know a thing or two. We need to take care."

"I'll be fine with those two harmless old ladies. But you're hobnobbing with the posh set, and I think it's more likely the folk up at the Manor House we should be afraid of. I wonder what skeletons they have in *their* cupboards?"

As Charity and Muffin left them, Feargal said, "Don't look so worried!"

"It's been nearly two weeks. The police don't seem to have come up with anything at all, have they? It's a worry."

"They're busy interviewing people about the attack at the meeting. They've got no evidence to go on for the murder, and they're sure the two crimes are connected."

"I only hope they're right and they're going to track this killer down soon. I'm getting to like some of those people - Julia, Sara, Jake .. even the nutty Major. I'd hate to think it's any of them."

"You know from last time round, that .. let's say people can surprise you."

So it was in a more sombre mood that they parted, and stepped back onto the bustling everyday Malvern streets and into the real everyday world again.

CHAPTER TWENTY-TWO

After lunch on Thursday Tamsin drove past the Bishop's Green cottages on her way to her lesson with young Bingo. She spotted Charity's little blue car outside the middle cottage, and smiled at the thought of the three elderly ladies regaling each other with stories from way back when.

When she arrived at Bingo's place, she saw Verena out on the road with the puppy on a lead, an empty plastic bag in her hand and an impatient expression on her face.

"Just trying to get him to poo before we start!" she called over as Tamsin pulled up in the drive. "No hope of that now you're here - look how pleased he is to see you!"

He was, and so was Tamsin pleased to see him, but didn't miss the opportunity to teach him to keep his feet on the floor while he greeted her.

"You're so clever, Tamsin! I never remember to do that. Oh, Mike's had to go and see someone, so you just have me today," she grinned.

"The more you remember, the faster he'll learn!" Tamsin chided gently. And as they went into the house she asked Verena how she was doing with the homework. But her hostess was far more interested in gossiping: "And *what* do you think of what's going on?"

"Let's have some fun with Bingo and talk after," she replied firmly, and got going with the lesson.

Verena couldn't wait for her chin-wag and slid the kettle over onto the Aga hotplate as soon as they finished.

"I hear that man Jackson is still off work," she began, as she clattered the cups and spoons.

"Apparently he'll be limited to outside work from now on. I don't think Lionel realised how much antagonism there was from his staff, and he sees now that that's not going to work for his new upmarket conference centre."

"How are the mighty fallen! He's always been quite snooty, I found."

"Jackson? I still can't see why he'd want to kill Torben though ..."

"Just jealousy over the girlfriend, I suppose. I doubt if he thought the environment people would seriously have any chance of stopping the project, so it can't have been that."

"And he's yet another person who knows how to wield a bow and arrow. It's a peculiarly Bishop's Green sort of murder!"

"I'm glad I've never had any interest in archery - at least it leaves me out of the frame," Verena agreed fervently. "Mike thinks it must have been some of those boys who go to the class - just fooling around."

"Surely not! They're quite young, aren't they? And someone did break in to steal the equipment. Maybe Mike's hoping it'll all blow over?"

"He has some dealings with the Council through his work. It seems the project is looking a bit rocky."

"Really? Maybe the cottagers will be safe after all?"

"We love this place," Verena thoughtfully stirred the cream in her coffee mug. "Hate to think of anything nasty here ..."

"Something nasty *is* here, though. We have to face facts."

Verena shuddered, looking very sad.

"But it doesn't seem to be a lunatic popping off arrows at everyone - you're probably quite safe," Tamsin went on. "Don't get too down - you have a lovely puppy to keep you happy! So let's look at what I want you to do with him this week .." Tamsin got the usually-bubbly Verena to focus on better things. She didn't like to see her so downcast.

Verena scooped up Bingo onto her lap while she studied the home-work sheets, and nodded as Tamsin circled some parts and underlined others. "Right you are, I'll work on those with this lovely little chappie. He's such a treasure - and so clever," she beamed proudly.

So Tamsin left her client feeling more cheerful, and as she came out of the house she heard the clopping of hooves and saw Sara riding down the road towards her.

"Hi Sara," she waved, "Hi Crystal!" Since their meet-up at Jeremy's cafe Sara seemed to have decided that Tamsin was one of the good guys, and she looked pleased to see her, hopping down to the road to chat. Tamsin was just reaching out to touch Crystal's velvety muzzle when the still day was pierced by a terrified, distorted, scream, making them all jump and causing the horse to skitter on the road and rear up.

"What was that?!" she said as she jumped out of the way and Sara calmed her horse. "It came from the cottages!" Tamsin's blood ran cold.

Another scream - louder than the last - galvanised them into action. Tamsin started to race towards the cottages while Sara steadied Crystal enough to mount her, get her onto the grass verge and canter the short distance down the road, overtaking Tamsin who was now puffing after her. By the time she arrived at the Damsons' cottage Sara had vaulted off Crystal and was tying her to the gatepost.

They ran into the house together to find Edith Damson lying on her back waggling her arms and legs like an upturned beetle, and Marjorie shouting at a furious Muffin who was pulling her backwards by her dress with muffled growls. She teetered unsteadily, arms flapping, then fell against the window ledge waking the dozing cat who spat and leapt off hissing, dodging between Sara and Tamsin's legs as it made its escape from the mayhem. Charity, still screaming, stood with a cushion clutched in front of her, holding it out as if to ward off evil.

Sara went to see if Marjorie was alright, while Tamsin clambered past all the furniture and sprawling bodies to reach Charity, who dropped the cushion and clutched onto her, sobbing. Tamsin held her close, making soothing sounds, and Charity's grip gradually loosened a little as the gasping sobs slowed down.

By now the room was full of people. Being the nearest neighbour, the Major had arrived next and was immediately taking charge. Jake followed his instructions, lifting the chubby Edith onto a chair, as Sara helped her scrawny sister Marjorie onto another. The sisters looked rebellious.

"Don't want you here,"

"No, don't want you here. Please go away."

"Away!"

Tamsin had settled Charity into the remaining chair and plonked Muffin on her lap. "Charity, tell me what happened?"

"They tried to kill me!" gasped Charity, and wrapped her arms round her little dog fiercely. "And Muffin saved my life!"

"Don't want anyone here," Marjorie continued.

"Please go away," said Edith.

"Tried to kill you?" said the Major, "How?"

"With that cushion," Charity, wide-eyed, pointed to the cushion on the floor as if it might rear up and attack her again. "They tried to suffocate me. Muffin pulled Edith off, so I snatched the cushion and screamed."

"Why?" said Tamsin, aghast. "Why would they do that?"

"We want you to go now, thank you." Edith stared ahead of her, apparently unseeing.

"We want our tea now," added Marjorie, her arms folded.

"I've called the police," said Sara, slipping her phone back in her pocket. Perhaps we should all have some tea while we wait for them. Calm everyone down?" and she headed for the kitchen, suddenly showing the maturity and capability of her mother.

"These ladies seem traumatised," said Major Cooper-Johnson, indicating the two sisters in their trance-like state.

"This one certainly is!" Tamsin sat on the arm of Charity's chair and stroked her hand and Muffin's head by turns. "I hope the police get here soon."

They didn't have too long to wait as the clock on the mantelpiece ticked relentlessly on. It was when Sara carried a tea-tray in to the now silent room and handed each sister a cup, that they heard the wail of the police car. The sisters were immobile in their chairs, and showed no sign of wanting to move. They just protested from time to time that everyone should go.

"I called an ambulance too," Sara said, "they sure look like they need medical attention."

"Do you need a doctor, Charity?" asked Tamsin.

"No thank you, dear. I'm beginning to feel better. They didn't hurt me - they didn't have time," and she buried her head in her little dog's fluffy neck.

By the time two uniformed policemen had arrived, larger than life, their jackets bristling with squawking walkie-talkies and badges and goodness know what else, the little parlour was full to bursting. They directed the Major and Jake to leave the room so the ambulance people could get in with all their kit. The quaint room which had seemed to belong to another century was transformed into a modern accident scene.

After a quick conference with the police, the paramedics loaded the two sisters into wheelchairs to get them out to the ambulance. "They look like frail old ladies, but you may need to use restraints," advised the sergeant, who was by now getting used to being called out to dramas in Bishop's Green - especially those involving Charity. "We'll come to the hospital to interview them as soon as we're done here."

And so, as his constable got out his notebook, he turned to Charity saying, "So can you tell us exactly what happened, Madam?"

CHAPTER TWENTY-THREE

"Everything was just fine," began Charity, "until I noticed that photo over there." She indicated the old black and white photo of a group of men in flying gear beside a Lancaster bomber that Tamsin had noticed before. "Apparently two of their brothers are in the picture, and they were killed in the War. So many bomber crews never made it back .." she shook her head sadly. "Anyway, I remember they'd said there were five children in this little cottage once, so I asked if there was a photo of the other child. And that's when they suddenly went mad." She reached out for Tamsin's hand again, and held Muffin close. "They started raving about how no-one should ever ask about him, that it was all so long ago, that - oh, I don't know - that I shouldn't pry into their past. I apologised and assured them I didn't want to pry, but it was too late - Edith grabbed a cushion and flew at me." She bit her lip and pressed Tamsin's hand.

"Take your time, Madam," said the Sergeant quietly, not wanting more hysterics.

"I didn't know what to do - I was being pinned back into this deep armchair and I couldn't breathe. But I just got out the word 'Pull!'"

"Pull?" The constable looked up quizzically, his pencil poised over his notebook.

"It probably just sounded like a muffled noise - but clever little Muffin understood immediately, didn't you Muffiepuff?" Muffin looked up and licked Charity's chin happily.

The Sergeant sighed and cast his eyes heavenward saying, "I wish *I* understood."

"It's Muffin's trick," Tamsin thought she'd better weigh in with an explanation. "When Charity says 'pull' Muffin grabs hold of whatever clothing is being offered and pulls. To help pull off a jacket, you see, or a sock. I guess the only clothing she could see was Edith's skirt flapping above her while she struggled to suffocate Charity, so she pulled her backwards."

"*Clever dog!*" said Sara, her eyebrows raised.

"Useful little animal," conceded the Major, now back in the room again.

"Oh I'd love to teach Bingo that!" piped up Verena, who had heard the sirens and all the commotion and arrived in the Damsons' front room as the ladies were being wheeled out to the ambulance.

"So then I was able to scream."

"And you screamed good-o!" laughed Tamsin. "I'm surprised Crystal didn't take off in the opposite direction!"

"We'll need you to come to the station to sign this statement Miss Cleveland, but for now I suggest you have someone take you home. You can collect your car another time. I do hope next time we meet it will be in less fraught circumstances," he smiled.

"Oh do come to me first - you can really relax before leaving," said Verena hopefully. "When Mike's back we can drive your car over to you. It's the least we can do. Er, is Muffin safe with a puppy?" she suddenly asked anxiously.

"Muffin loves all dogs and all people," said Tamsin with a smile, as she helped Charity emerge from the depths of the armchair, "except perhaps for those attacking her mistress!"

And so while the Major directed Jake what to clear up in the house and took charge of locking it up, Tamsin and Charity adjourned to Verena's home. Sara needed to calm Crystal, who'd managed all the bee-baws and flashing lights splendidly but was quite on edge, and continue her ride - "to settle her," she explained.

"Another cup of tea?" queried Charity, now ensconced on a comfortable sofa in Verena's living room - a chair she'd be able to escape from - as her hostess started to assemble the tea things.

"Oh yes, and lots of sugar. There's cake too. You've both had a shock."

"You can say that again!" Tamsin shook her head ruefully. "It seems Bishop's Green doesn't agree with you, Charity."

"I'm not sure I ever want to come here again, you're right, my dear. Though I think Muffin's enjoying her visit," said Charity, watching Muffin play so gently with young Bingo, allowing the puppy to take turns at 'winning' the game. She leant back against the cushions and closed her eyes. "I'm beginning to feel a little better."

"Watching these two play is a comfort to anyone - you relax there while I help Verena."

And once they were all enjoying the cake, they began to puzzle over what had set the Damsons off.

"I've never heard of another brother," said Verena as she topped up Charity's cup. "Wonder what happened to him."

"I asked about the third brother when I visited, and they said he'd emigrated to South Africa."

"Lots of young men did at that time," said Charity reflectively. "After the war - all that excitement - some found it hard to settle down to normal life again."

"So *I* asked. Then *you* asked. Perhaps you were the last straw Charity?"

"Either way, it's pretty weird they should react like that. Whatever can have possessed them?" said Verena.

"It was so sudden." Charity shuddered, and Verena reached her hand out to her. "It was as if a switch flipped."

"You know what?" Tamsin sat up in her armchair. "I'm going to get Feargal to do a bit of digging. I bet he can find out about this brother - whether he actually did go to South Africa. Perhaps he was a ne'er-do-well and was banished, his name never to be spoken again!"

"And the Africa story was a smokescreen?" asked Verena.

"Maybe he never went," Tamsin said.

"Maybe ... he never left." added Charity slowly.

"Oh my. You think he might be the one those anonymous letters were about?" Tamsin gasped. Verena looked puzzled, but Charity had already begun replying.

"Well, if you remember, I was going to find out if there'd been a previous death, maybe a long time ago. I asked them what they knew of that in a very roundabout way. And now I'm wondering .."

".. if their brother did die, and they thought you were on to them?" Verena jumped in.

They all sat in stunned silence for a few moments, the silence broken by play-growls and grunts from Muffin and Bingo, who were now pulling each end of a rag toy.

"Look, Muffin is teaching Bingo her trick!" Verena laughed.

Tamsin smiled then said, "That could certainly explain why they reacted so violently to your innocent question about the third brother."

"If it's a secret they've been keeping all these years," said Verena thoughtfully, "I imagine it's frazzled their minds."

"And Charity, how did they respond to your question about a previous death?"

"Now you mention it, there was a certain coldness. They looked at each other. I remember now - while Edith said she had no idea what I could possibly be referring to, Marjorie changed the subject and started talking about her cats."

"I think we're on to something. Thank you so much for having us, Verena, and most especially for your offer with the car. Let's get Charity and Muffin home, and I'll set things in motion straight away."

Tamsin jotted down Charity's address on the back of her business card and gave it to Verena. "I've been racking my brains, and I remember now, his name was Simon. When Marjorie told me his name I immediately had an image of a black and white spaniel - my childhood dog," she smiled self-deprecatingly, "he was called Simon."

"Simon Damson. That should give you plenty to go on!" Verena jumped up and clapped her hands excitedly, like a schoolgirl.

And helping Charity up and aiding the two dogs bring the game they were enjoying to an end, Tamsin led the way to the door.

"We should be able to drop the car over later - or tomorrow morning at the latest. Is that ok?"

"Most kind," said Charity, handing her the keys. "I must say I do feel very tired now .."

Tamsin hurried her along to the van, and immediately buzzed a text off to Feargal. She wasn't to know then that she'd opened a floodgate, and things started flowing very fast.

CHAPTER TWENTY-FOUR

On Friday Tamsin was up to her ears in home visits - puppies were sprouting everywhere, and people seemed so ill-equipped to manage them when they arrived. "Still, that's my bread and butter," she smiled to herself, as she left one happy client's house having transformed life for their puppy, who hopefully wouldn't be hearing nonono again.

So it was much later in the day before she got a chance to catch up with Feargal. He'd sent her a couple of texts, the first saying that there was never a passport issued to Simon Damson of Bishop's Green, and the second, a few hours later, saying there was no record of his entry to any of the then British colonies in Africa.

She was sharing some supper with Emerald when the dogs announced that a car had pulled up in Pippin Lane. Feargal appeared at the back door and waded through the dogs, bristling with excitement.

"You have to hear this!" he said, helping himself to a slice of bread and butter. "Do you mind? I'm starving! Haven't stopped all day."

Emerald gathered together a plate and adding some cheese and tomatoes to the bread and butter she dished up more food for him. "Here, food for the warrior," she smiled.

"I've got to thank you Tamsin," he said between mouthfuls. "That was an amazing scoop you handed me!"

"I saw you'd been working on it all day."

"I have. And you won't believe what has happened." He took another mouthful of food and waved his hand while he munched hungrily. "This is delicious! Just give me a moment ..." and he hoovered the rest of the food up in jig time.

Tamsin and Emerald grinned at each other and had to contain their impatience until Feargal was ready to hold court.

"First of all, there's no record of Simon Damson after he was demobbed in 1946. No passport ever issued. No entry visa of any kind to any of the African colonies as they were then. Nothing. Put that together with the anonymous tip-off and it seems he may have come to a sticky end. I found an old report in a paper about his father, drunk and disorderly, fighting in the street, with other offences to be taken into account. So it seems he may have been a ruffian - perhaps a bully. They didn't investigate 'domestics' in those days. The strange demeanour of the two sisters would confirm the influence of a bully in their lives. They sure are twisted up ..."

"True enough. They seemed to me to be off with the fairies when I visited." Tamsin chipped in as Feargal drew breath.

"My 'mole' as you call him -"

"Ah, so it's a 'him'!"

"I'm afraid I think of moles as male," Feargal smirked as he went on, "but don't jump to conclusions!"

"My *mole*, of whatever sex, says they're being interviewed in the presence of social services - to advocate for them: they're clearly nuts. But separating them for questioning has helped get nearer the truth."

"They can't do their Pat and Mike act."

"Their what?" asked Emerald.

"Irish expression. They repeat each other all the time, finish each others' sentences, continually validate each other." Tamsin filled her in.

"Weird!"

"Weird is right," Feargal continued. "And when the police mentioned the development, that's when one of them freaked out. Seems they're terrified of the land being disturbed - dug up."

"Oh no!" chorused Tamsin and Emerald, grasping the significance of this straight away.

"So our intrepid Inspector Hawkins immediately dispatched a team to their garden, equipped with metal detectors and some geo-phys specialists and their equipment provided by the archaeology department at the university."

Tamsin and Emerald waited, mouths open.

"And they found him. Or, at least, they found someone. Buried in the vegetable patch. So it's now a crime scene - which is hugely exciting all the locals - and the remains have been sent to your chum Maggie for appraisal."

Tamsin sagged. "Those poor women. Imagine! For eighty-odd years they've been living with this knowledge. That their brother is buried a few yards from their house."

"No wonder they went batty!" said Emerald.

"And no wonder they stuck together! Never married, never left," added Feargal.

"*Couldn't* leave, I suppose. Do the police think they did it?"

"Too early to say. Lots more questioning will have to be done. But it seems likely that their father killed him and buried him. The girls would have been very young. They must have known - or at least suspected. Ghastly."

"Like I said before, there's a huge advantage in having a nosy social welfare system. Things could so easily be kept secret back then." Tamsin sighed.

"It wasn't the done thing to pry. What people did behind closed doors stayed there," agreed Feargal. "But you do see what this suggests, don't you?"

"Roland!" said Emerald. "Roland was snooping about with a theodolyte and his geophysical equipment the Major had explained to them. Maybe they thought he was actually from the developer and was measuring up in order to start digging! But they realised that one way or another, their secret would be out. He'd kind of x-ray the ground and find … what they've now found."

"Exactly. And, ladies, I think we've cracked both cases," Feargal folded his arms and leant back in his chair, smiling at Tamsin.

"Really?" asked Emerald. "The Misses Damson murdered Roland? How? What do they know about archery?"

"They're old country people. Look at Jake. What does he do to augment his larder?" replied Feargal.

"He poaches," Tamsin nodded.

"And a bit of hunting was always part of everyday life for rural people in the old days. Gleaning, culling, poaching, whatever you want to call it. They would have known how to kill an animal - learnt it at their father's knee. Good way to despatch a creature silently. Just the swish of the arrow in the dark .." With a whoosh sound he released an imaginary arrow from an imaginary bow.

"But how? Surely someone would have noticed them carrying a bow around the place?" protested Emerald. "They're quite big, aren't they?"

"Ahh," Tamsin gazed into the middle distance and smiled. "I got it! Julia told me they would go out every day with their ancient pushchair to gather firewood, or berries or whatever. Is that it?"

"That's it. It was Marjorie who went hysterical and spilled the beans about her fear of the land being dug up. But apparently Edith has remained stone-cold calm. She told the whole story."

Tamsin and Emerald leant forward expectantly in their chairs, elbows on the table.

"They would go out walking every day to collect things from the hedgerow, as you say, and take their antiquated pushchair. Probably the one they were pushed around in as children. They stole the bow and arrows from the Major's open shed one night, and kept it ready for use. It takes a while to set up a recurve bow - you have to connect all the bits, and you need a bit of strength for stringing it, but between them they could manage it - so they'd have to do it at home together, and transport it to where they wanted to use it. They'd put some branches - bits of firewood - in the pushchair to hide it. No-one who saw them would have been any the wiser."

"You're suggesting they made a practice of this?" asked Emerald.

"That time Roland appeared at Verena's," Tamsin thought out loud, "white as a sheet and terrified. Maybe he thought he was imagining things - two elderly ladies, dressed alike in old-fashioned dresses, pushing a creaking old pushchair .."

"And taking potshots at him with a bow and arrow!"

"You'd wonder, wouldn't you?"

"It looks like that's what happened. And it's possible the new crime scene will yield more secrets as SOCO - the scene of crime wallahs - work it over."

"Poor Roland! And he was trying to prevent the development all along!" Emerald clapped her hands to her head.

"From the garbled bits they got from Marjorie, it seems they had no idea of that till Major Cooper-Johnson was chatting with them after the murder, and told them that Roland had been on their side. Once they realised their mistake, everything fell apart. They'd been living on their nerves ever since. Easy enough for them to flip when Charity appeared to be on to them."

There was a silence while they all absorbed the horror of this.

"They thought he'd come to unmask their secret."

"Two old ladies, driven mad by guilt and secrecy," said Tamsin.

"For so many years!" said Emerald.

"For so many, many years," echoed Tamsin.

"Now you sound like the Damsons!" Feargal laughed, trying to lift the mood.

Tamsin and Emerald laughed too. "This must be what they call gallows humour!" said Tamsin. "But it's just pure relief, really."

"So these apparently innocent and harmless old dears killed that young man, and tried to kill Charity too. What's going to happen to them?"

"Honestly? I don't think it'll ever come to trial. They're obviously not fit. And they'd never be able to prove which of them fired the shot. I guess they'll be locked up somewhere for their remaining years. Now, how about one of your excellent coffees?"

So the three friends fell to relaxing together, playing with the dogs and Opal, to help them assimilate and process the awful story, as they felt the burden of fear lifting from them.

CHAPTER TWENTY-FIVE

Lionel was marching back and forth in his large kitchen. "Now they've got those old bats locked up, we can start looking forward again."

"Have you reconsidered your Conference Centre Manager, darling?" asked Felicity tentatively.

"Jackson's obviously not up to it. Expected too much of him. He'll stay on the estate work now. Tore him off a strip about that nonsense at the Village Hall. I'm watching how he treats the men more closely now. Thought I could trust him ..." He sucked his teeth thoughtfully. "I need to find the right man for this job - it's too important to mess up."

"Or the right woman?" asked Sara, idly pushing a morsel of toast round her plate.

"Exactly!" said Felicity, clapping her hands together. "A woman would do it just as well."

"Or better," smiled Sara.

"That gives me an idea ... my niece Lucy. Remember her, Lionel? She's been studying hotel management and whatnot at some place in Hereford. She'd be ideal."

"Actually, that's not a bad idea," said Lionel, returning to the table and pouring himself more coffee. "She's always seemed a capable gal. Give me her number."

"Glad that's settled! I'm going to go and get ready, Mum," said Sara, taking her plate to the dishwasher and tossing Grouse the leftover toast.

"Where are you off to?" asked Lionel.

"Warwickshire," said Felicity as Sara left the room. "They've got an open day at the rural college there."

"I thought she was going to university? Study something sensible?"

"Oh, this *is* sensible - it's a very highly-thought-of college. She wants to study conservation - woodland and wetland management. And the thing about this college is that she can take Crystal with her!"

"They take the horse too? Won't it cost us a fortune?"

"Not only will it not cost us a fortune, but she *is* your only daughter! And taking Crystal means one less job for us here."

"Woodland management, you say? Hmm, maybe she'll be useful here one day," he said grudgingly. "C'mon Grouse, time to walk the paddocks."

Felicity gave him a long look, as Sara came back into the room in time to see Grouse hop up and wait politely for Lionel to open the back door. "Tamsin's done wonders with that mutt," she smiled.

"She did a lot for the village too," Felicity added quietly as she watched Lionel and Grouse walking past the kitchen window on their way out to the estate. "Apparently she's done this before - solved a murder, I mean. Quite extraordinary."

"I had no idea! There must be something about working with dogs that gives her special powers of perspicacity," Sara smiled.

"You spend plenty of time communing with Crystal."

"Yes, I've always been more attracted to horses than to dogs - they just seem to speak to my soul. I'm dying to get to this college, Mummy - imagine working with trees and horses all day long. They do a lot of dressage there - I'd love to have a go at that!"

"I suppose dressage is the horse equivalent of dog tricks. Doesn't Tamsin do tricks with dogs? I seem to remember that's what saved her friend's life - her dog performing a trick at the vital moment?"

"She does, you're right. I'll ask her about it. If she can get dogs to pull off socks I'm sure she'll have some ideas for teaching Crystal to prance. I mean, you're right, dressage is just tricks after all."

"She's been dubbed Tamsin the Malvern Hills Detective, I heard. The *Mercury* ran a story on her."

"Ooh, where?"

"Over there on the shelf."

Sara snatched up the paper. "I'll read it in the car!" Then she turned back to her mother: "Are you going to prime Lucy before Dad rings her?"

"Yes, I'm going to make sure to do that today."

"I think it's a great idea! You'll have someone young about the place. Keep you company."

Felicity smiled fondly at her daughter. "You're right. I'm going to miss you."

Sara wrapped her arms round her mother before pulling away with a sniff. "You know I'm still so sad about Roland." She fiddled with the strap of her bag for a moment, then brightened. "But have you heard the news about the development?"

"No?"

"I was talking to Verena - her Mike has some connection with the council. It seems that they're going to insist on affordable housing being provided at the same time. New council policy to keep villages alive, or something. That's not going to give the developer enough profit, so we're hoping he'll abandon the project!" She grinned in triumph.

"I have to say I do like those quirky old cottages," confessed Felicity. "But don't tell your father. Let him vent his anger on some other messenger."

And smiling conspiratorially, they headed out for their exciting day.

CHAPTER TWENTY-SIX

Tamsin was enjoying a new sensation when she headed out on training visits to the part of the county around Bishop's Green. It was pure relief. Relief that the horror was over. She hadn't realised she'd felt so tense and haunted till the feelings of anxiety stopped with those awful revelations of a few weeks ago. But the relief was also mixed with pleasure - that she'd had a part in nailing the killer, or killers in this case.

And of that she was very proud! She still felt bad that she'd unwittingly sent her old friend into the lion's den - but they couldn't possibly have known. "All's well that ends well," she said to Quiz, who was accompanying her today. "And how about an orchard walk, Quizzy?"

Quiz opened her mouth in a smile as her tail wagged expectantly. She'd picked up the magic word 'walk'.

"We may be lucky and bump into Maggie and Jez. I've missed her the last few times I've visited the orchard. I'll buzz her a text. Let's hope she's free today!"

And, prophetically, she was. *Just back,* she had replied, *be there in 20 mins.*

While they were on their second circuit of the huge orchard, Maggie's car pulled up and she waved cheerily as she came towards

Tamsin. Jez and Quiz renewed their acquaintance with some gentle sniffs and they all started walking.

"I gather this is never coming to court, so how can I get the gory details," asked Tamsin.

"I can tell you, off the record. If it turns up in the *Malvern Mercury* I'll know who passed it on!"

"Don't be too sure of that. Feargal's a good investigative journalist."

"Ok, point taken. So here's what we learnt. It seems that Simon died of a crushing blow to the side of the head, in keeping with a punch with a fist. But he also had previous badly-healed injuries, mostly juvenile."

"Oh the poor fellow. How ghastly."

"During the war, where his brave brothers were killed, he didn't see active service. His eyesight was poor, so he captained a desk for the duration. We can never know, but it's possible he just didn't measure up to his dead hero brothers in his father's eyes. And as by all accounts he was a drunk and a bully ... "

"I get it. Poor boy. It seems that man has a lot to answer for."

"Lots of lives ruined, by the demon drink. His son, his daughters, a young man ... "

"His wife must have had a bad time of it. Seeing all this going on and being powerless to stop it."

"No evidence has come to light of her collusion, it's true. But as the case is shelved we'll never get to find out. Perhaps she was bullied into silence. He probably knocked her about too." They walked a few steps deep in thought till Tamsin snapped out of it and tossed a pine cone for her dog to snuffle out of the undergrowth.

"Here Quiz!"

"And there have been other developments," Maggie said, as Quiz ran back with her prize.

"Oh?"

"Yes, a load of bow and arrow parts have landed on my desk. They found them at the Damsons' cottage. The metal bits - the arrowheads and the risers - were in the ashes of a bonfire."

"Oh Lord. That just about seals it, then."

"I think it was pretty cut and dried already, by their own confessions. That just confirms it - ties up loose ends."

"Where are the old women now?"

"A secure asylum. Can't see them ever getting out, to be honest."

"So sad. But! I have some good news."

Maggie paused to remove a teasel from Jez's tail, and looked up smiling as she tossed it away, "Tell all!"

"A couple of Sara's environment friends are taking the Damson cottage. And the great thing is they're taking on all the cats too."

"I didn't know there were cats. What happened to them these last few weeks?"

"Jake's been feeding them. The guys are delighted with their furry housemates! Oh, and Pru is home again with her chickens - she's the one at no.4. She missed all the excitement while she was away, and is making up for lost time in chatting to everyone - she's nice! Her son Tom is keeping a low profile now. He was keeping his ear to the ground round the cottages to see if he could benefit from the proposed development. But now that's dead and gone, he's got other fish to fry."

"People do show their true colours, eventually," mused Maggie. So Jake is relieved of his cat-minding duties?"

"And his chicken-minding too. He was looking after Pru's chickens, in return for the eggs of course. Actually I dropped in there a few days ago, to stock up. His produce really is very good. You should drive over there and sample it."

They walked on some more paces. "I was just filling a large bag with courgettes, saladings, and strawberries. I had Moonbeam with me, you know - my little terrier. Jake appeared while I was picking my purchases from his table - he usually keeps out of the way, like a shy deer. Well, he looked straight at me and tipped his hat. 'Fine terrier,' he said, nodding to Moonbeam. It was the most I've ever heard him say!"

"I reckon he's glad you helped solve the mystery."

"I think so. Of course I had nothing to do with the development cancellation. And you can feel the relief in the row of cottages. Now they know they're staying, they're all making sure their front gardens are spick and span. There's Julia's floral jungle, the Major's safari park, the neat front garden at Pru's, Jake's productive and orderly patch, with his table and little handwritten signs."

"And no.3?"

"Roland's friends are tidying it all up nicely. At this time of year a garden can grow to look abandoned very quickly. But it looks neat enough now, with plenty of shrubs for the cats to bask under. And the lads are getting on well with the Major. They're helping to research those water beetles that started it all off. Right up their alley."

"Nice to have someone younger there, too."

"They are young, yes. And enthusiastic. I saw them playing football with Oliver and Romeo on the Green the other day, with Francine in goal between two jackets rolled up on the ground, looking bored as only a teenage girl can! I still go that way to work with Grouse and Bingo."

"That's Verena's puppy, isn't it?"

"Yep. And they tell me Sara got her place at that college - she *and* her horse! She can't wait to go."

"Goodness! How do they fit the horse in the lecture hall?" laughed Maggie.

Tamsin enjoyed this happy feeling - of walking in the beauty of nature, with two lovely dogs and a friend, and not a care in the world.

"Life is wonderful," she said out loud.

"It is indeed," agreed Maggie.

"Hey Maggie - tell me, would you be free for a while tomorrow afternoon? Will you be working in Malvern tomorrow?"

"I will be as it happens. What have you in mind?"

"There's a little event happening at The Cake Stop. It'll be fun! Be there about 3."

"I'll look forward to this mysterious event," smiled Maggie, "especially as it's likely to feature good coffee!"

CHAPTER TWENTY-SEVEN

Three o'clock the next day found a rowdy group in The Cake Stop, with Jean-Philippe and Kylie ministering to them.

"*Encore!*" said Jean-Philippe delightedly. "Once more we celebrate your success at bringing low the murderers!"

"Well it wasn't just me," protested Tamsin, settling her dogs on their beds in the space in front of the tall window. "Feargal did all the legwork .."

"And Charity was the star!" put in Feargal, smiling fondly at Charity and Muffin, ensconced in the largest armchair The Cake Stop could provide. It was so big that Muffin was able to sit comfortably beside the diminutive old lady.

"I just happened to be in the right place at the right time," she responded modestly, turning to beam at Muffin.

"Or the wrong place at the wrong time!" laughed Emerald, who had found a place on the sofa with Moonbeam on her lap, next to Maggie.

"You're in the right place now!" Jean-Philippe assured her, as the door opened and in came the three Furies carrying cake-boxes.

There was much excitement as Penelope bustled about issuing orders in her stentorian voice and organising her troops, and their newest Peach and Raspberry Pavlova - with lashings of whipped cream - was unveiled by Electra. And amidst all the congratulations and delight, Damaris stepped forward and opened the smaller cake box, bringing out what appeared to be a miniature Pavlova with chunks of watermelon on top.

"This one is for the heroine of the piece," boomed Penelope, "for Muffin, for extreme valour in the face of the enemy!" There was a smattering of applause and some cries of "Go Muffin!" and "Yay Muffy!"

"Oh, it's lovely," stammered Charity and blushed slightly. "But I'm not sure she should have all that cream and sugar?" She turned to Tamsin questioningly.

"I think you'll find it's a dog-friendly cake," smiled Tamsin quietly.

"We took advice from the expert!" Penelope declared to the whole cafe.

Damaris tapped each finger in turn as she said, "It's liver cake, covered with cream cheese and decorated with sprats and watermelon."

Feargal stuck out his tongue and pulled a disgusted face, "Yuk!"

"It's not for you, chump!" laughed Emerald.

"But you're right Charity," Tamsin continued unfazed "it'll be very rich, so not too much at once."

"It's just as well we have several brave dogs who'll be able to enjoy it! I can vividly remember what they did .. last time." Charity nodded to Tamsin's dogs in the window.

Kylie appeared with a tray laden with a stack of plates and a large knife, their coffee orders, hot chocolate for Charity, and tea for Dodds and Co Cakemakers - as the Furies were officially known.

Penelope, as ever, stayed in charge, marshalling her troops to dish up huge slices of the gateau onto plates and hand them round. Damaris stood with knife poised over the little cake, "How much should I give them, Tamsin?" and together they put different sized helpings of the special cake onto paper plates ready to give to the dogs who, to their credit, were sitting patiently where they'd been put, waiting to see if there was anything for them - albeit with a few drips from their mouths.

Once all the people were served with their cake and their drinks, Tamsin stood and said, "We're here today to honour a very brave person and her very brave dog. But for Muffin's swift and effective action, we could be attending a very different gathering." She paused for this horror to sink in. "So let's give the dogs their cake, and enjoy our party!" And so saying a laden paper plate was put down on the floor in front of each dog, who all looked at Tamsin waiting expectantly. "Gettit!" she said, and they each dived on their plate, making short work of the treat, accompanied by smiles and much laughter from the rest of the party.

Once they were settled again on their beds and laps, Banjo happily demolishing his plate into shreds as he got the last of the cream cheese, the rest of the guests started on their cake. And once they'd all enjoyed it, with forks being scraped on plates so as not to miss any of the peachy creamy goodness, Feargal tapped a spoon against his mug and called for attention.

"We know Tamsin is a remarkable dog trainer, getting quick results in the kindest possible way." Everyone looked at Tamsin, now blushing a goodish pink. "But she's shown herself to be very astute at understanding the human species too. Her curiosity - perhaps triggered by her curiosity about how dogs' minds work - leads her to unravelling mysteries like the one we were recently faced with. And like last time, she found herself drawn into the investigation in order to clear a name. Last time it was her own name. This time it was her friend's name. But there is something irresistible about Tamsin on the warpath for justice."

There was a murmur of agreement, and Maggie chipped in, "Chief Inspector Hawkins looks like the cat that got the cream! Though officially he'll say civilians should keep out of police matters, he's secretly very happy that this one got cleared up so quickly."

"Well," continued Feargal with a smile, "I've greatly enjoyed working with Tamsin - with her shafts of insight,"

"And Emerald's shafts of insight," interrupted Tamsin.

"Yes, the shafts of insight coming from Pippin Lane are remarkable. I'd love to carry on collaborating with you Tamsin - but do you think you can stop stumbling over dead bodies?" Feargal sat down amidst the applause and laughter, and the curious attention of the other customers in the coffee shop.

"I think we shouldn't be disturbing everyone else," Tamsin began quietly, "but I do want to say that there were a lot of people instrumental in leading us to the truth in this case. Some are here and some are not. Like, the environmental protesters were actually on to something; care for nature and our surroundings and rural values won the day; and who'd have thought there was an underground coffee shop network?"

Jean-Philippe gave a Gallic shrug, "*Mais, oui!*" and tapped his nose knowingly.

"But what I mean is, it wasn't just me. I just happened to tie it all together, I suppose. And nothing would please me more than to be able to give a dog training lesson without this kind of drama!" she laughed. "Since your lovely article in the *Mercury*, Feargal, the phone hasn't stopped ringing. I'm really going to be too busy doing what I love to do any more detective work. But, I have to say, I've met some splendid people over the last few months, and it's been a privilege to know them - including, of course, all of you here."

She smiled happily at them all, and as Electra jumped up to serve more cake to everyone. picked up her fork and said, "Now, for once, I'm going to have seconds!"

TO FIND *out how Tamsin arrived in Malvern and began Top Dogs, you can read this free novella "Where it all began" at*
https://urlgeni.us/Lucyemblemcozy
and we'll be able to let you know when Tamsin's next adventure is ready for you!
Want to read the first book in this popular series? You'll find it at
https://books2read.com/Cozy1 And here's your QR code >>>>

^^^ Scan the code above or click here to read Book One *Sit, Stay, Murder!*

And if you enjoyed this book, I'd love it if you could whiz over to where you bought it and leave a brief review, so others may find it and enjoy it as well!

ABOUT THE AUTHOR

From an early age I loved animals. From doing "showjumping" in the back garden with Simon, the long-suffering family pet - many years before Dog Agility was invented - I worked in the creative arts till I came back to my first love and qualified as a dog trainer.

Working for years with thousands of dogs and their colourful owners - from every walk of life - I found that their fancies and foibles, their doings and their undoings, served to inspire this series of cozy mysteries.

While the varying characters weave their way through the books, some becoming established personnel in the stories, the stars of the show are the animals!

They don't have human powers. They don't need to. They have plenty of powers of their own, which need only patience and kindness to bring out and enjoy with them.

If you enjoyed this story, I would LOVE it if you could hop over to where you purchased your book and leave a brief review!

Lucy Emblem

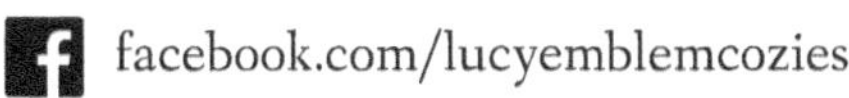